"What's keeping you awake? Maybe talking will help."

Ethan doubted it was going to help either of them sleep if he told Crissanne he'd been consumed with images of her. That he couldn't stop thinking about her mouth and wondering how it would feel under his. He rubbed his hand over his chest as his skin started to feel too hot, too small for his body. He needed her.

He knew what lust felt like, but this was more.

This was Crissanne. Not a stranger, not someone he could simply hook up with and then smile goodbye at the next morning.

They had history.

And on his side...attraction.

So much wanting, he thought. In the moonlight, with the shape of her body hidden by the flowy nightgown she had on, his imagination was running away. He wanted to lift the hem of that gown—

"Ethan?"

Yeah, this had bad idea *written all over it.*

* * *

Craving His Best Friend's Ex is part of the Wild Caruthers Bachelors series from Katherine Garbera.

Dear Reader,

I grew up in the '80s and loved Rick Springfield and his song "Jessie's Girl." I think it's safe to say that I wanted to be Jessie's girl and have Rick singing about me with such longing in his voice. So when I was thinking about Ethan Caruthers and the woman he lusted after, I had the chance to write about that feeling. Crissanne is Ethan's best friend's ex-girlfriend. Unlike the song, she was never Ethan's but she could have been...if only Ethan had asked her out when he'd first seen her instead of pointing her out to his best friend.

Love is complicated. I think we all know that. Nothing rational dictates whom we fall in love with or don't fall in love with. Sometimes the person who seems so perfect for someone else actually doesn't end up having those feelings. But in Ethan's case, he sort of liked that Crissanne was out of reach. He could have that perfect/ideal love in his head and it wasn't messy or complicated...until she shows up on his doorstep alone and single.

I really had a lot of fun writing this book and I hope you all will enjoy coming back to Cole's Hill, Texas, and catching up with all of the Wild Caruthers men!

Happy reading,

Katherine

KATHERINE GARBERA

———

CRAVING HIS BEST FRIEND'S EX

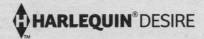

Recycling programs
for this product may
not exist in your area.

ISBN-13: 978-1-335-97169-2

Craving His Best Friend's Ex

Printed in U.S.A.

www.Harlequin.com

USA TODAY bestselling author **Katherine Garbera** writes heartwarming and sensual novels that deal with romance, family and friendship. She's written more than seventy-five novels and is a featured speaker at events all over the world.

She lives in the UK with her husband and Godiva (a very spoiled miniature dachshund), and she's frequently visited by her college-age children, who need home-cooked meals and laundry service. Visit her online at katherinegarbera.com.

Books by Katherine Garbera

Harlequin Desire

Sons of Privilege

The Greek Tycoon's Secret Heir
The Wealthy Frenchman's Proposition
The Spanish Aristocrat's Woman
His Baby Agenda
His Seduction Game Plan

The Wild Caruthers Bachelors

Tycoon Cowboy's Baby Surprise
The Tycoon's Fiancée Deal
Craving His Best Friend's Ex

Visit her Author Profile page at Harlequin.com, or katherinegarbera.com, for more titles.

To the Zombie Belles for having my
back and making me laugh!
It's hard for me to believe that I've known
some of you more than 20 years!
I love you all.

One

Ethan Caruthers opened the door to find Cris-sanne Moss standing there, face pale, biting her lower lip the way she did when she was worried. What was she doing here? She had her camera bag flung over one shoulder and a suitcase on the step behind her, and a taxi was pulling away from the curb. She pushed her sunglasses up on her head, and a strand of her silky, straight long blond hair slipped free in the late summer breeze. She parted her lips and blew the strand away. As always, he had to force his eyes away from her mouth.

With some women he'd met, he could easily ignore the fact that they were female. But from the moment he'd been introduced to his best friend's girl, it had been a struggle to control his intense attraction to her.

He had felt so disloyal to Mason yet at the same time had been powerless to control his attraction. He'd wanted her from the moment he'd seen her and he'd hesitated…

"Well, hello there. I wasn't expecting you, was I? I mean, Cole's Hill, Texas, isn't your normal neighborhood," he said, holding the door open for her to enter before going to get her suitcase. She'd been living in LA with his best friend, Mason, for the better part of the last three years.

"No, you weren't expecting me, and when you hear why I'm here I won't blame you if you tell me to hit the road," she said.

Crissanne had a Northwestern twang to her speech that he'd always found endearing. He couldn't imagine anything she could do that would make him send her away. "I'm a lawyer and have heard some pretty outrageous things over the years. I doubt you'll shock me."

She gave him a sweet smile that didn't reach her clear gray eyes and then reached over and hugged him. "You've always been the best, Ethan. Frankly, I didn't know where else to go…"

Intrigued, he put her suitcase against the wall

near the front hall table and then closed the front door before turning to face her again. He wanted to ask where Mason was, but also thought he remembered something about his best friend heading to Peru to film his extreme adventure survival show.

And right now, Ethan was pretty sure he was going to hell for lusting after Crissanne, but he'd never been able to look at her and not see the two of them tangled together in a big king-size bed.

He liked to think that he'd hidden his reaction, though; he was always on guard whenever he was around Mason and Crissanne.

"Come into the kitchen. My housekeeper made some sweet tea and chocolate chip cookies before she left for the day," he said. "We can have a snack and you can tell me why you're here."

He gestured for her to precede him down the hall. It was the gentlemanly thing to do, but as his gaze fell to her hips, which swayed gently with each step she took, he knew there wasn't anything polite about his attention. He wanted her. He swallowed hard and knew he had to get himself under control.

He'd broken up with the woman he'd been seeing off and on in Midland a while ago, so he'd been celibate for longer than he liked. "I need to grab my phone from my study. Help yourself to the cookies."

He turned into his study and then stood there for a second, forcing himself to remember everything he'd ever heard in Sunday school about not coveting things that weren't his. He grabbed his smartphone from the desk and then went down the hall, sure he had himself under control, until he saw her standing at the French doors that led to his back porch, resting her head against the glass.

She looked lost.

She needed a friend.

He remembered the hug and it was suddenly easier to shove his lustful thoughts to the back of his mind. She needed him.

"Crissanne?"

She turned and pulled her sunglasses from her head, putting them on the kitchen table. She put her hands in her back pockets, which thrust her breasts forward in the loose, peasant-style top she wore.

Damn.

"Mason and I broke up," she said, her words pouring out in a rush. "We had a really bad fight and he said I could stay in his condo in LA while he's in Peru but I couldn't. I…I just needed to get away. And I don't have any family. When I got to the airport I didn't know where to go, and then I thought of you."

But he was stuck on *Mason and I broke up*.

She was single.

She was hurting and alone. He knew she had no family. She'd grown up in the foster system and had only a few close friends…most of whom she shared with Mason. They'd been a couple since freshman year in college. Clearly, she needed Ethan to be her friend at this moment. Something he'd always been for her. And he buried his desire for her as he always did.

"Of course you are welcome to stay here as long as you need to," Ethan said to put her mind at ease right off the bat.

"Thank you. Honestly, I know this might put you in an awkward position, but I didn't know where else to go."

He shook his head. Of course it was going to be uncomfortable to explain to Mason when his friend called. But turning her away didn't sit well with him. It was easy to say that his dad had raised him to be a gentleman—and it was true. Crissanne was in a tight spot and clearly needed a friend. But the truth was he *wanted* her here and he'd endure anything to have her under his roof. "It won't be awkward. Are you sure this is a permanent breakup? I know Mason gets moody before he goes away to film."

He wanted her to be happy, and until now he'd thought she and Mason were the ideal couple. As much as he wanted Crissanne for himself, her happiness had to come first. And Mason might be an ass when it came to women, but over the years he'd noticed that they seemed good for each other. Mason had been the one to encourage Crissanne to set up her travel vlog, which had turned into a financial boon for her and given her a career she was in control of.

"I'm sure. He and I have grown apart lately. And I know he's your friend so I'm not going to talk smack about him to you, but we want different things out of life."

That was news to him. Obviously. But he'd sort of avoided hanging out with them too much lately because it had become too hard to be around Crissanne and not want her. Business had brought him to the West Coast more frequently and as dinner plans with Mason had fallen through because of his shooting schedule, it had been just Ethan and Crissanne. And he had hated that weakness in himself.

"Do you want to talk about it?"

She shook her head, long strands of hair sliding over her shoulder to rest on the curve of her breast. "Not right now."

"Well, how about I show you to your room and you can clean up, and then I'll treat you to dinner? I didn't have my housekeeper prepare anything."

"That sounds great," Crissanne said. "Are you sure you don't mind?"

"Positive," he said.

"I'll start looking for my own place right away," she said. "LA was always Mason's town and I'd been thinking of living in the center of the country instead of staying on the West Coast…so it's here or Chicago, and since I know you…but I can definitely stay at a hotel. In fact, I should have gone there."

"Stop. You can stay here. There's no hurry for you to find a place. This house is big enough for both of us," he said. And Mason would be out of the country for a few weeks, so Ethan had time to figure out what to say to his best friend when he got back home.

"You really are the best friend a girl could ask for," she said.

He tried to tell himself that he could settle for being friends, but it had been a lie for a while now, and he knew that having her in his home was going to make it even harder.

* * *

Crissanne had hoped for this reaction from Ethan. She'd be lying if she said she hadn't noticed that Ethan had always had a little crush on her. She had hoped he'd take her in. She wasn't the kind of woman who made friends easily. Part of it was because she was competitive, but also she'd never really learned to trust. She remembered how the psychologist her last foster family had sent her to when she'd turned eighteen had stressed that this was going to be a barrier to her happiness.

Maybe it was what had driven the wedge between Mason and her. But the truth was, she had nowhere else to go. She'd rung her friend Abby, who lived in San Francisco, but she'd just started a relationship with a new guy and thought it would be weird if Crissanne moved in with them.

She had a good relationship with her brand manager at one of the large luggage brands that sponsored most of her vlogs and gave her most of her work, but she didn't want to call her up and ask to live with her. She had needed a friend and someone who wouldn't judge. And Ethan was that.

Also, he was busy. As an attorney, he was in court a lot so she'd have some quiet time to figure out what was next. She would make this work. Because staying in the house she'd shared with Mason after that horrible fight where things were said that could never be taken back was something she simply hadn't been able to do.

She wanted to be someplace where she felt accepted and Ethan always made her feel like she was someone. Not a girl who had been abandoned by her crack-addicted mother or passed from foster home to foster home because she was too quiet and weirded people out.

"This is your room," Ethan said when they reached the second-floor landing and he opened the third door on the right.

She stood in the doorway of one of the most luxurious bedrooms she'd ever seen. She'd never visited Ethan before; he'd always come to the West Coast. The house had a lot of Spanish design influence, from the tiles in the entryway to the large sweeping arch that led into the great room, but this room had more of a rustic Western feel. The carpet was thick and lush, and as she stepped into the room she wished she'd taken her shoes off so she could feel it on her bare feet. A large four-poster bed with dark navy drapes and a canopy on it dominated the space. The nightstands on either side of the bed each had a lamp. There was a sitting area with two overstuffed leather armchairs, a small table between them, and a landscape painting depicting the Texas Hill Country on the wall.

"This is a gorgeous room," Crissanne said.

"Glad you like it. There's a desk in the alcove over there leading into the walk-in closet and then to your private bath," he said, gesturing toward them. "If you need anything at all just let me know."

"I'm really low-maintenance, so I don't think I'll need anything," she said.

"Hey, you know, I bet once Mason lands in Lima he's going to be on the phone apologizing," Ethan said.

She didn't think so. Mason couldn't get away from her fast enough when she'd suggested maybe they should get married and think about a family. She'd expected him to balk a little, considering their life together was meetings in airports and nights together in the different apartments he owned in major cities around the world. But the outright rejection had stung.

When they'd talked, he'd said he didn't want to have a family...well, that had changed things for her. A family of her own had always been her dream, especially after her rough, lonely childhood.

"I wouldn't count on that," Crissanne said.

"Well, like I said, you're welcome as long as you need to be here," Ethan said. "Take your time settling in. I'm going to be in my study working.

I have to be in court early tomorrow and want to go over my notes again."

"We can skip dinner if that would be better for you," she said.

"No. I was planning to eat out. And my daddy would kick my butt if he knew I served you cereal after you came halfway across the country," Ethan said with that crooked grin of his.

"How are things on the Rockin' C?" she asked.

"Not too bad. Dad is retired but that doesn't mean anything to him," Ethan said. "He still sticks his nose in all the time, making Nate crazy."

Ethan was one of four brothers. Nate was the oldest. He'd taken over running the family ranch, the Rockin' C, and was the CEO of the company that had interests in oil and mineral rights. Another of his brothers, Hunter, was a former NFL wide receiver who had recently been exonerated in a scandal that dated back to college. And then there was Derek, who was a surgeon in Cole's Hill.

Ethan was way too sexy to be an attorney. She felt no guilt whatsoever in thinking that. He had thick, dark blond hair that curled onto his forehead despite the fact that he had styled it to stay back. His tailored shirt hugged his frame, showing off his muscled arms and hugging his lean abdomen.

"Does he make you crazy, too?" Crissanne

asked, realizing she'd spent too much time staring at Ethan.

"At times," Ethan admitted. "But luckily Nate's daughter, Penny, is a good distraction. Having a granddaughter kind of calms Dad down. So it's not just me here at the house in addition to my housekeeper. I have a…manservant. Saying that makes me feel way too *Downton Abbey*, but *butler* sounds pretentious as well. Anyway, his name is Bart and he lives here and takes care of the house, the pool and the yard."

"You need two helpers to keep your house?" she asked.

"I probably don't need them but I am gone a lot. And Bart needed a job and no one would hire him because he had a record. Mrs. Yarnall used to work for my parents until they moved into the small house and didn't need her anymore. Now that it's just Nate at the Rockin' C, there isn't a need for two housekeepers at the main house. She has five or so more years before she retires, and I could use the help here."

"Weren't you worried about hiring Bart?" she asked.

Ethan shook his head. "He's a good man who just grew up with bad influences. And I've seen a real change in him since he was paroled."

If she needed a good example of the kind of

man Ethan was, this was it. He cared about everyone. He saw the person, not all the other junk like upbringing or record or age. Not that many people took that kind of time to really make sure everyone had a purpose the way he did.

Though she'd come here knowing he sort of liked her, she didn't kid herself that it would turn into something more than just curiosity. Mason was his friend, and Ethan was loyal. Not blindly loyal, but the kind of man who lived by his own code.

Then again, he probably had been crushing on her because she was forbidden fruit. And that made her sad, because she wanted Ethan to be the perfect man she always imagined him to be.

He strode toward the door and then hesitated. "The balcony overlooks the pool and grounds. It connects to the other rooms," he said.

"Where is your room?" she asked.

"Two doors down," he said before leaving and closing the door behind him.

She stood there in the nicely appointed room, trying very hard not to feel like she was lost. It had been a long time since she'd had this feeling, but she was flashing back hard to the foster homes of her youth and feeling adrift, like she wasn't sure where she was going next. She was on her own again. She'd gotten used to being part of a family with Mason, and she knew that it had been a false feeling. He'd liked the noncommittal state of the relationship, and she'd been able to fool herself that it was something else. Something more. And she promised herself she wouldn't do that again.

Rubbing the back of his neck, Ethan entered his study and closed the door, leaning back against it. His brothers were all settling down and getting their lives together, but what did he have in his life that mattered? One thing was his job, the career he loved and would never give up. And the other was a woman who thought of him as her friend.

Hell and damn.

He walked to his desk, sat down in the big leather chair his mom had helped him pick out, and glanced down at the photo of him and his brothers that had been taken at Nate's wedding. His life always looked ideal, perfect from the outside. And that had made him struggle.

He knew his weaknesses and never shied away from them. So he knew ignoring this thing with Crissanne wasn't the solution. He had to face it, deal with it and then let it go.

He'd texted Bart earlier to let him know that Crissanne was here. Ethan wondered if they'd met and introduced themselves yet.

He left his office, following the sound of music

playing to the kitchen. Not Bart's usual MO, but perhaps he'd been charmed by Crissanne, too. There was something about her, a sadness lurking in her eyes, that had always made Ethan want to cheer her up.

But Bart wasn't in the kitchen. It was just Crissanne, singing to Jack Johnson while she sat at the island typing on her laptop. Her back was to him, and he stood there watching her.

He tried to tell himself it was sweet, that there was nothing remotely sexy about her as she worked. Yet she still tempted him. He decided then and there that the only solution to this was to try to think of her like one of his sisters-in-law.

She glanced up from her work and turned slightly. When she saw him standing in the doorway, she stopped singing.

"Sorry," she said. "I guess I got carried away and was singing out loud."

"You were," he said. "I liked it."

"You did?"

"You don't sound nearly as bad as Hunter. That boy has a lot of talents but singing isn't one of them," Ethan said, thinking of his younger brother, the former NFL football player.

"Your family always sounds so…"

"Big and annoying?" he asked.

"Nice," she said at last. "I don't have any siblings."

Ethan leaned back against the countertop. "They can be a pain in the backside. I can't tell you how many times I wished I were an only child."

"But you don't still feel that way?"

He shook his head. He was glad he had his brothers and that he lived so close to his family.

"I was thinking while you are here, you might want to do a feature on Cole's Hill for one of those travel blogs you write for in addition to doing your vlogs. We have the SpaceNow and NASA Cronus training facility here now. I marked them on a map for you while I was in my office," he said, going over to the desk in the kitchen and picking up the map he'd drawn for her.

He handed it to her and she arched both eyebrows at him. "You seem to have put a lot of time into this."

"It didn't take much time," he said. "I figured you'd want to keep busy. I know that's how I felt in the past when my relationships ended."

She arched an eyebrow at him. "I thought you were the one-night man."

"No need to ask where you heard that," he said. Mason always called him that. "I've had a few relationships that lasted longer."

"I kind of want to dig into that and find out why you never let yourself get involved for longer," she said, then winked at him. "But that would be too prying."

"It would be," he agreed. He'd have to make up something if she did try to probe more deeply, because she was the reason he'd never gotten involved with anyone for the long term. It had never seemed fair to get involved with one woman when he was obsessed with another one.

She gave him one of her sweet smiles and then came around the counter and hugged him. He held himself stiff at first but then put his arms around her and hugged her back, even knowing that he shouldn't. He closed his eyes and breathed in the flowery scent of her hair, and then forced himself to step back.

"I'll let you keep your secrets for now," she said.

"Should I say thank you?" he asked.

"Yes," she said.

"Ready to go to dinner?"

She nodded. "Let me get my bag and phone."

She walked out of the room and again he watched her go, knowing he was fooling himself pretending to be her friend. He was good at arguing a point in court and convincing juries to believe his point of view, but he'd never been able to bluff himself. He had always been very aware of his own weaknesses and if he was being completely honest, Crissanne felt like a dangerous vulnerability. There was no way he was going to ever be able to look at her and not want more, not want to feel her lips under his and not want her body twined with his all night long.

Two

The Peace Creek Steakhouse was conveniently located near the downtown area of Cole's Hill. When Ethan was growing up, his family would rent the wine room in the back to celebrate major accomplishments. As he and Crissanne stood in the foyer waiting to be seated, he remembered how he'd get money from Babs, one of his parents' housekeepers, to get mints from the machine in the front of the restaurant and how he and his brothers would all scramble to be the first one there.

It was in his childhood that Ethan learned to

argue with his words and not his fists. He was never going to be stronger than Nate, who was two inches taller than Ethan. But Nate could be distracted by anyone who didn't share his point of view. Of course, some of those early arguments had ended in a broken nose for him. But it had been worth it to be the first to the candy machine.

"What are you thinking about?" Crissanne asked.

He shook his head. "Fighting with my brothers to be the first to get a mint from that candy machine."

"It's so foreign to me that you've lived in the same place most of your life," she said. "I bet everywhere you go there are memories."

"There are," he said. "Don't you have places where you could go back to?"

"I guess," she said. "The group home I lived in as a kid was torn down a few years ago, and then as a teen I was in a home in Northern California, but I hated it. I felt so…out of place in my Goodwill clothing. I think I'm better at looking to the future," she said.

He started to reach out to squeeze her shoulder but stopped and dropped his hand. Desire had always been such a part of the atmosphere when he was around Crissanne. With Mason as a barrier to anything ever actually happening, he'd allowed himself casual touches that were much more dangerous now. He needed to be careful.

She was still off-limits, but it didn't feel that way.

"That's the best way to look at it," he said. "You can't change the past."

She moved away to look at the pictures on the wall while he gave their name to the hostess, who was the daughter of one his cousins, Liam Shannon. He exchanged small talk with her as she promised him the first table that was available and then moved away from the hostess stand. Ethan had never noticed the framed prints before. They were all images of cowboys that were at least thirty years old, which he knew because there was one of his father when he'd first inherited the Rockin' C, standing in front of his F-150 pickup with the Rockin' C logo. His dad had been the one to take the ranch to the next level of production. The family company had the mineral rights that earned them a large part of their fortune, but Winston Caruthers had made the cattle ranching operation a contender in the portfolio.

"This guy… I love the mixture of confidence and bravado in his eyes," Crissanne said as Ethan joined her.

"That's my dad," Ethan said. "One of his sayings is 'he who hesitates is lost.' He's always just gone for whatever it is he wants."

She turned to look at him. "You have inherited that. You never hesitate, do you?"

One time.

When he and Mason had both seen Crissanne across the quad and he'd stood there wondering if he should ask her out, while Mason, always willing to take a chance, had stridden over and done just that.

His dad was right.

Again.

He took a deep breath. "I have my ups and downs."

"Seems to me that you have more ups than downs," she said. "Your business is very successful."

"Usually, but I don't like to brag."

She mock-punched him on the shoulder. Damn, her touch sent an electric current through him, even though he realized she was still touching him like a friend. He had hesitated…damn, he'd done it again. She rattled him.

He prided himself on being calm and in control, but she was messing with his restraint. He didn't like it.

If he'd learned anything in his thirty years on

this earth, it was that he didn't do well without some sort of limits.

A strand of her hair fell forward, and he lifted his hand to tuck it back behind her ear. Her lips parted and she caught her breath. He couldn't help rubbing his finger down the side of her neck—her skin was so soft—before he dropped his hand.

"Ethan…"

"Yes?"

"Mr. Caruthers," the hostess called. "Your table is ready."

Crissanne swallowed hard and then nodded and stepped around him to follow the hostess into the dining room. The dynamic had changed between the two of them.

He had changed it. He'd tried to be casual about touching her, but there was no way he could continue to hide the way he felt, especially now that Mason was out of the picture.

And while a part of him knew that caution would be the noble route, another part of him didn't care about that, the selfish part that could only see the woman he'd always wanted walking in front of him to a table set for two. Her hips swayed gently with each step, her blond hair swinging back and forth as he watched.

But they were friends.

At least that much was true. He thought about

his brother Derek and his best friend, Bianca, and how they'd somehow managed to turn friendship into love. But that wasn't him and Crissanne. It had never been the two of them in their friendship; it had always been three of them. And it would be ridiculous to think that Mason wasn't going to come to his senses and return for her.

Ethan knew that was what he'd do.

So tonight had to be two old friends catching up…nothing more.

Crissanne fell back as Ethan engaged in a conversation with one of the many people in Cole's Hill who knew him as they walked out of the restaurant. It was safe to say he was a favored son here. She saw in the bones of the streets and its charming historic district that it had been a small-ish town but was growing quickly. In fact, the man who was talking to Ethan was discussing a development going in just south of the town limits.

Her fingers itched for her camera. She used the one on her smartphone at times, but she preferred to have the lens at her eye, fiddling with the focus until she could capture whatever it was about her subject that fascinated her.

Maybe if she did that, then she'd be able to understand this attraction to Ethan she was feeling. But she wasn't holding out hope that it would help.

The light from the storefront of the Peace Creek Mercantile was throwing shadows on his features, bringing that strong jaw of his into focus. *What the heck.* She took her phone from her pocket and opened the camera app.

The light played over his hair, drawing her eye to the fact that he had some light blond highlights. She tuned out everything, watching Ethan through her camera app and moving to get the right angle for the photo. She zoomed in closer, and saw he had a scar on his left eyebrow…she'd never noticed that before.

His expression was earnest and confident as he focused on the man he was talking to. That was one of the things she really liked about Ethan. He gave his attention 100 percent to whomever he was engaged with. She snapped a few photos, but when she moved around to change her angle, she bumped into someone.

"Sorry."

She glanced up to see a cowboy. Like a legit, thought-they-only-existed-in-the-movies cowboy. He had a leonine mane of brownish-blond hair streaked through with gray, his eyes had sun lines around them, and his skin was tanned. Leathery, she'd say, but he wore his years well. There was something familiar about the set of his eyes and his nose. She knew it would be rude to snap a picture of him, but that face told a story.

"That's okay. I'm sure you could find something prettier to photograph, though."

"Than what?" Crissanne asked.

"That shark over there. You know he's the type to argue," the cowboy said. "He's a lawyer."

"I know," she said. "He's a champion at debating just about anything. One time we spent forty-five minutes arguing the merits of fresh salsa versus that stuff they serve at the fast-food chains."

"Surely there was no competition," the cowboy said.

"Believe it or not, he thought that the fast-food salsa had its place on the salsa scale."

"That boy always was ornerier than a mule," the cowboy said.

"Only someone who knows Ethan well would say that," she replied. "Who are you?"

"Hello, Pa," Ethan said, joining them. Then he turned to Crissanne. "I told you my family could be a pain."

"You did," she admitted.

"Winston Caruthers," the cowboy said, holding out his hand. "You can call me Pa—everyone does."

Crissanne knew it was a casual offer, probably

one he made a dozen times a day, but she'd never had a father figure. No man had ever offered for her to call him Pa. And it meant more than she knew it should.

"Thank you," she said, taking his hand. "I'm Crissanne Moss."

"Pleased to meet you, Crissanne," Pa Caruthers said. "Ethan, you'll have to bring your girl out to the house one night soon to meet your ma."

"Pa, uh, we're not a couple. She's Mason's—"

"Ex. I'm Mason's ex and I'm here for a job, so Ethan is letting me stay with him for a few days. We were friends in college," she said, taking control of the conversation. She had no idea what Ethan had been about to say, but Crissanne knew she wasn't Mason's anything anymore.

"Your ma would still like to meet her," Pa Caruthers said in a firm tone.

Ethan's jaw tightened. "Of course."

"As I said, Pa," Crissanne interjected, and it gave her a little thrill to say it, "I'm working here so I'm not sure what my schedule is, but we'll try to get out there."

Winston nodded and put his hat back on. "See you on Saturday, Ethan."

"Yes, sir," Ethan said. His father nodded at Crissanne and then moved on down the sidewalk.

"He still thinks I'm a teenager," Ethan said.

"I think it's sweet," she said.

Ethan arched an eyebrow at her. "Sweet? He's ornery as hell. Everyone says that."

"Do they also say you're just like him?" Crissanne asked, because he sounded just like his father had when he'd been talking about Ethan.

Ethan chuckled. "Yeah, but that doesn't mean they're right."

"Did you get some good pictures of the town?" he asked.

She flushed. She was pretty sure all she'd photographed was Ethan. "I did. Sort of scene shots with the street and the people on it."

"Good."

They continued walking in silence back toward Ethan's Ferrari, which he'd parked at the far end of the historic district on the other side of the Grand Hotel. She thought about how nice this town was, how lovely Ethan's family was and how she really had to be careful about her emotions. This was a stopgap. Cole's Hill was meant to be a place for her to breathe and then figure out her next move.

She couldn't fall for the town or the Caruthers. And she knew that was a distinct possibility. Ethan held her attention—Lord knew, he always had—but seeing him here and not in Los Angeles was bringing him into focus.

And she wished she could say that she was seeing all his scars and his faults, and that was a turn-off. But his scars made her understand him better. Which was dangerous. She could resist perfection. But she was going to have to really stay on her guard to keep the Ethan she knew at arm's length.

Ethan had been in bed for two hours listening to the sound of the wind blowing and the scrape of the tree branches against his window. He really needed to take care of that. But he knew that wasn't what was keeping him awake.

Crissanne was in his house. Sleeping just down the hall in the spare room. He had never slept with her under his roof before. It wouldn't have mattered before, but now he knew it did.

He'd told himself over and over that she was just a friend.

She was still Mason's girl until his best friend told him otherwise.

And of course that just sharpened the ache of desire inside him. His skin had felt too tight for his body all night, except for those few moments when she'd smiled at him, and then he'd forgotten she wasn't his. She was here as a friend. And she was her own person.

She'd come to him for friendship, and he was going to deliver.

He rolled over and saw the empty expanse

of the bed next to him. He closed his eyes and swore he smelled the scent of her perfume drifting through the open French doors that led to the balcony.

He got up and walked to the open door and saw the shadow of someone standing at the railing.

Crissanne.

He reached for his jeans and drew them on over his naked body. He carefully pushed his erection out of the way as he buttoned his jeans, and then scrubbed his hand through his hair as he stepped out.

"Couldn't sleep?" he asked, keeping his voice low so he didn't startle her.

"No. Too much in my head," she said, turning to face him. She wore a thin sleeveless nightgown that ended at her knee. The moon was full tonight and it shone down on her, making her look almost as if she wasn't of this world. As if she didn't belong here.

Hell.

He knew she didn't.

"Did I wake you?" she asked, leaning back against the railing. The breeze stirred her hair, catching it and making it flow against her shoulder and then across her face. She tucked it back behind her ear.

"No."

"I'm glad," she said. "But what's keeping you awake? Maybe talking will help."

He doubted it was going to help either of them sleep if he told her he'd been consumed with images of her and that he couldn't stop thinking about her mouth and wondering about her kiss. He rubbed his hand over his chest as his skin started to feel too hot. He needed her. He knew what lust felt like.

But this was Crissanne. Not a stranger, not someone he could simply hook up with and then smile at the next morning.

They had history.

And on his side...attraction.

So much wanting, he thought. In the moonlight with the shape of her body hidden by the flowy nightgown she had on, his imagination was running away from him. He wanted to lift the hem of that gown—

"Ethan?"

"Huh?"

"Do you want to talk about it?"

He shook his head. "No. What about you?"

"I definitely don't," she said.

"Want to play sips and lies?"

She laughed. "The last time we played that I won."

"Only because I let you," he said.

"Uh, sure."

"It's true," he called back over his shoulder as he walked to the wet bar at the end of the balcony. "I'm a gentleman."

"Whatever you say," she said, moving over to the padded lounge chairs that were clustered around a portable fire pit. She sat down and pulled the throw off the back of the chair, drawing it over her shoulders.

He busied himself looking through the bottles searching for the Patrón that he knew was her favorite. And then he sliced a lime and put it on a serving tray next to the shaker of salt and two shot glasses.

He set the tray on the end table between two of the chairs. "Are you cold? I can light the fire."

"I'm okay with the blanket," she said, pouring both of them a shot of tequila.

"Who's going first?" she asked.

"You."

"The gentleman thing again?" she asked.

He shook his head. "Haven't had time to think of a lie that you'll believe."

She started laughing.

He loved the sound of her laughter. He still remembered the first time he'd heard it all those years ago. She'd been sitting on the arm of Mason's chair and someone had said something and she'd started laughing. It was such a joyous sound it always made him smile and at times had cut through the fog he'd allowed himself to live in for a few years.

The game, which they'd played many times in college and since then, was simple. They took turns telling a story and the other players had to guess if it was true or false. If the guess was right, the one telling the story had to drink, and vice versa.

"Topic?" she asked.

"First kiss," he said. It was the first thing that had come to his mind, and as soon as he said it he knew that he was in trouble. He shouldn't be sitting in the moonlight with Crissanne, drinking and talking about kisses. He didn't have the strength that he'd need to keep his distance.

"First kiss? Well, that's an interesting one. It was that time I kissed a frog," she said. "I was at this party at school and I remembered the fairy tale about the kiss turning a frog into a prince. Molly Moore dared me to do it, and I thought what the heck and did it."

He leaned back in his chair. "Was the frog an actual amphibian?"

"What other kind is there?" she said, not really answering his question.

"I'm going to go with lie," he said.

"Truth. I got in trouble for kissing the frog and had to have detention," she said.

"Why?"

"Molly and I were really there to free the frogs from the science lab, so me kissing one was the distraction while she set the others free."

Their eyes met as he licked the back of his hand and shook some salt on it before licking it off again. Then he tossed back the shot, keeping eye contact with Crissanne, before he brought the lime wedge to his mouth and bit it, the tangy juice filling his mouth.

As he tossed the used lime wedge onto the tray, Crissanne reached forward, brushing her thumb over his lower lip and sending a jolt straight through him as she pulled her hand back and licked her thumb.

Yeah, this has bad idea written all over it.

Three

It was August in Texas, so even this late at night it was hot, or at least that was the excuse Crissanne was going to use for the heat sweeping through her. It had nothing to do with the fact that Ethan sat across from her wearing a pair of low-slung faded jeans and nothing else. His chest was bare, and he had more muscles than she'd expected.

He was a lawyer. Surely that meant he spent a lot of time at his desk not working out. But to be fair his muscles weren't overly large...just enticing. He had a flat stomach but no washboard abs, so realistically she knew that there were probably women somewhere in the world who would argue that he wasn't the sexiest man alive. But sitting here in the moonlight with the taste of lime on her tongue and his warm voice telling her a tale that she knew was a lie, she knew she wouldn't agree with those women.

He arched one eyebrow at her and she realized he'd stopped talking.

"Uh…lie?"

"Woman, you are wrong," he said, handing her the bottle of Patrón. And given the fact that her judgment was already a little off-center, she knew she should call it a night and go back to her bed.

Instead she took the tequila and poured it into her shot glass. Their eyes met as she licked the back of her hand, and she noticed that his pupils dilated. She shook the salt out, then leaned forward as she let her gaze drop and licked the salt, watching him from under her eyelashes. She noticed the muscles of his chest contracting as she tossed back the shot and felt the sting of it before she took the lime and bit it.

She put the lime on the tray as Ethan got out of his chair and walked to the balcony railing. She watched him as he braced his hands on the wrought iron and craned his head forward. His back was long and smooth, his neck strong and sexy. That intense longing rose inside her again.

And all the reasons she thought she had for coming to Texas floated away on the night breeze. She watched Ethan, felt the conflict inside him and knew she should go back into her room.

But instead she got to her feet and went over to him. She wrapped her arms around his waist and then leaned her head against his back right between his shoulder blades. He went tense for a minute before he relaxed.

"This is a bad idea," he said, his voice a low rumble that carried no farther than her ears.

She rubbed her hand over his smooth chest, and she knew he was right as she kept her face buried between his shoulders. But she'd been alone for a long time. Even though she'd only just broken up with Mason, they'd been drifting apart. She hadn't spent more than a few hours with him in the last six months, and she knew a big part of her had already started to move on.

She didn't want to think about that. About how easy it was for her to lock away her hurt and disappointment and just function. She had thought… well, hoped that she'd left that in her past. That the girl who had never connected with any of the families she'd fostered with had grown into a woman who made solid bonds with her boyfriend.

It hurt to realize how wrong she'd been.

"I don't care," she said. Saying it out loud made

her realize it was true. "There is something between us."

He took her arms from around him and stepped aside.

"Yeah. Mason."

She shook her head. "That's not what I meant. I always had you pegged as a straight shooter, but I guess you are probably used to saying whatever you have to in order to win an argument."

He shook his head. "Don't do that."

"Do what?"

He closed the gap between them in two long strides and reached for her, his hands briefly brushing over her shoulders before he dropped them to his sides.

"Don't make this impossible," he said.

"It already is," she said. "Or maybe I'm the only one who feels this."

He shook his head. "Dammit. You know you're not."

He stepped closer, and the waves of heat from his body enveloped her as he reached for her waist and drew her closer. She put her hand on his arm, and felt his biceps tense as he lifted her slightly off her feet.

He lowered his head toward hers, and she tipped hers back. Their eyes met. A flash of their entire history went through her mind. All the times they'd sat quietly talking in a corner while Mason had been entertaining their friends with some daring trick.

She knew that this was sudden and was afraid that Ethan would pull back. That he'd let his friendship with Mason keep them from kissing. So she did it.

She initiated the kiss.

His lips were warm and firm, but soft. When they parted, she tasted the lime and tequila on his tongue as it rubbed over hers.

She dug her fingers into his upper arm and lifted her head trying to get closer to him. He tasted good. His kiss was perfect, and so was the way he held her to him. She felt him shift so that he was leaning against the balcony railing, her body resting fully along his.

She felt his hard-on against her lower stomach, and her breasts were nestled against his chest. Just the thin layer of her nightgown kept her from feeling his skin against hers, and she wanted more. She let her thigh fall to one side so that his leg was between hers, and he groaned as his hands roamed down her back to her butt, cupping it and shifting her into a deeper contact with him.

She raised her head to look down at him, and he was watching her. Just staring up at her. She wasn't sure she could read the emotion in his eyes, but it sparked something deep inside her that was more than sexual need.

She started to draw back, aware that she was craving something from him that felt dangerous and edgy, but he tunneled his hands in her hair and drew her head back to his.

Her hair was soft. Way softer than anything he'd touched recently. Her eyes were half-closed, lips wet and swollen from their kiss. Her hands were on his waist, holding him lightly. She tipped her head to the side, their eyes met, and he thought of all the arguments he could make. All the reasons that he could list to make himself drop his hands and walk away from her. But he wanted her.

And he'd been denying it for too long. It had been easy when she lived with Mason, but now that she was here in his house, sitting on his balcony, putting her hands just inches above his groin, he knew he wasn't interested in anything other than following his gut instinct, which was clamoring for him to pick her up and carry her into his bedroom.

"Are you sure?" he asked. He had to. This was Crissanne. She meant more to him than a hookup.

And it didn't matter to him if it wasn't the same for her. She might be looking for sex from him just to forget or to make Mason jealous or for a million other reasons. But for him this was the one woman he'd wanted for over a decade. The one woman he'd thought he'd never touch like this. And he needed to be sure she wanted him, too.

"Yes," she said, her fingers moving up the center of his body until she wrapped them around his neck and kissed his chin and then his jaw.

He stopped thinking. His mind shut down and he turned his head to capture her lips with his. His grip on the back of her head tightened a little bit as he tried to control the passion that was roiling through his veins.

She was unleashing something that he'd forgotten was a part of him. He groaned and then wrapped his arm around her hips, standing up and carrying her into his bedroom without breaking the kiss. He stepped over the threshold, and she pulled her head back.

He let her slide down his body, biting back a moan at how good she felt against him. And then he realized she might change her mind now.

Hell.

He would have to let her go if she did.

But please, God, don't let her change her mind.

He watched as she trailed her fingers down his chest again, and then glanced over her shoulder at the king-size bed that dominated his room. The studded-leather headboard was mounted on the wall and there was a huge pile of pillows that his housekeeper arranged each morning when she made the bed. Above the bed were the horns of the first longhorn bull he'd raised when he was a kid.

"I always forget you're a cowboy," she said, turning to look at the horns.

He shrugged, taking her hand in his and drawing her closer to his bed. "Not really, but I can put on my boots and cowboy hat if you want me to."

"Only if you lose these jeans first."

"Uh, I don't think any self-respecting cowboy would be seen like that," Ethan said.

"Too bad," she said, raising both eyebrows as she stepped back and let her eyes move slowly over his body. "You'd look damn good in just a hat and boots."

He felt his chest swell and he couldn't keep his pecs from flexing. "You think so?"

She nodded. "Maybe one day…"

"Maybe," he said. He wasn't sure he'd do that. He was a lawyer. He was the serious Caruthers brother. The arguer who was always thinking of the consequences. Which couldn't be said of him tonight, as he stood there in his bedroom next to Crissanne with a raging hard-on.

She turned back to him, her hair swinging around her shoulders as she held her hand out to him. He took it, lacing their fingers together, and she stood on her tiptoes and put her hand in the center of his chest again, spreading her fingers out and rubbing her palm over his skin. A shiver went through him and he drew her closer. He lowered his head, but this time it was just so that their foreheads would meet.

He felt the brush of her exhalation against his neck and closed his eyes.

Crissanne Moss was in his bedroom.

All the feelings he'd been ignoring flooded him, and he realized he wanted this to be more than it could be. He wanted sex, of course; he couldn't deny it. But he wanted her to somehow be his.

And that wasn't what was happening.

This was a hookup. He knew it.

For her, this had to be rebound sex. Something to prove to herself she was still attractive.

He knew because he'd had a dozen hookups like this. Where he was sleeping with someone else to prove that he was over her. Over Crissanne.

And now she was here, and he knew that he was willing to be whatever she needed him to be tonight. He was done with pretending that he didn't want her.

He cursed under his breath, and she shifted her head to the side, putting her finger over his lips.

"Don't think," she said.

"Is that the only way you can be here with me?" he asked.

She cursed, and he realized that he wasn't going to do this.

She didn't know how to answer Ethan's question. Of course, the whole situation felt like trouble no matter how she sliced it up. She wanted him. She wanted to be with him. She had narrowed down the list of people she could stay with to him. And now she was in his bedroom trying to convince herself that she could get with him and then be cool the next day.

But even with her skill at ignoring her emotions, that sounded like an impossible situation.

"No. Not like you mean," she said. "It's just if we start to think, then we're going to be back to pretending that we don't want each other. And that's a lie. I'm tired of pretending with you, Ethan."

"You say that but you were with my best friend," Ethan said.

"That's over."

"Is it? Or is this about making him jealous?" Ethan asked.

Was it? She hadn't even thought about Mason when she'd gotten on the plane. She'd been thinking of the one person who'd always made her feel better.

"No. Honestly, there are men a lot closer to LA who would have fit the bill if that was my goal. I'm here with you…even though this is what I wanted to avoid. And once we start talking it's going to get complicated."

He sighed and then stepped back from her, walking over to the bar in the corner of his bedroom and then pouring himself something that looked like whiskey from where she stood.

"It was complicated before we started talking," he said quietly. "We were both just letting our hormones direct us."

"Was that so bad?" she asked.

"I don't know. The thing is, Crissy, I don't want either of us to wake up in the morning with regrets. And as good as tonight would feel I know that we would."

"Why is nothing easy?" she asked out loud. But really she wanted the answer from herself. "I'll leave in the morning. I saw an ad for a B and B in the ladies' room at the restaurant tonight. I should have gone to a hotel or something."

He just watched her, the whiskey glass in his hand. As he stared at her she felt the emotions coming off of him, but she was too turned on to think about how it was impacting him. She was embarrassed that they hadn't just fallen into bed, and dealing with everything else was just beyond her tonight.

What was it that caused these men in her life to pull back? What was it she lacked? She couldn't even get the man who'd looked at her with lust in his eyes when he thought she wasn't paying attention to sleep with her.

She was broken in some way that the world picked up on. She hadn't realized it until this moment, and if she were a different person, one who actually allowed herself to connect to her emotions, she knew she'd be crying.

. But instead she just turned and walked out of his bedroom, past the fire pit and the discarded shot glasses and limes, and tried not to think about how the fun they'd had earlier had turned into this mess.

She entered her bedroom and walked over to the bed, sitting down on the edge, rubbing the back of her neck. She couldn't stay here.

Not for another second.

She wondered at the pattern of her life that every time she ended up in a place she wanted to be, she ruined it and had to leave. This was a new record for her. Not even twenty-four hours.

Stop.

She forced herself to move.

No thinking.

The words that had changed everything in Ethan's bedroom now motivated her to get up and get dressed. She pulled on a pair of jeans and the first T-shirt she touched. Then she got her suitcase from the closet and put it on the foot of her bed.

Her phone vibrated and lit up on the nightstand, but she ignored it. She wasn't in the mood to read her news updates. She had enough on her plate right now.

She went back to the closet but her phone was blowing up with messages, vibrating like crazy. She walked over and glanced down at the screen, seeing they were from a number that wasn't programmed into her phone. But based on the area code, she thought it might be the production company that Mason worked for.

Unlocking her phone, she opened the text messages and began reading them with a mounting sense of disbelief. Then she let the phone fall from her fingers as she sank to the floor, drawing her knees up to her chest.

Mason's plane had crashed.

Oh my God.

She hadn't thought she had anything left to feel, but she hadn't been ready to say goodbye to him. She immediately tried to call Mason. His phone rang, and then a message came on saying that he was out of range and to try her call again later.

She texted the production company back, asking for more information. But there was no immediate response.

She hadn't realized that until this moment a part of her had been holding out hope that he'd come back to her. It made her feel small and stupid, because she'd thought she was over him. That she'd buried those emotions so deep, pretending she didn't feel them. But they were there.

"Crissanne."

She glanced up to see Ethan standing at the foot of her bed. His phone was in his hand and his face was pale. She stood up and ran over to him.

"Did you get the message?"

"Yeah. I can't get through to Mase or the guy who sent the text," Ethan said.

"Me, either," she admitted. "Do you think he's okay?"

"I don't know. We both know he can survive a lot. He's got skills."

"Yeah. Skills."

Ethan opened his arms and she closed the gap between them, putting her head against his shoulder and just crying. She didn't know what to say.

Suddenly she was very glad she hadn't slept with Ethan. Not tonight. Not now when Mason was...

"Do you think he's dead?" she asked.

"I hope not."

Four

The next morning, after a mostly sleepless night when Crissanne had dozed off and on and Ethan had just watched her, they were both in his home office trying to get answers. Sitting in the guest chair, Crissanne looked smaller than he'd ever seen her. All that bravado she usually presented to the world was gone. She had one of the cashmere throws that his housekeeper placed on the back of the chairs over her shoulders.

Ethan was at his desk on his laptop, messaging with the production company and trying to use his contacts in South America to see if they had any local information. So far, all they knew was that Mason's plane had gone down near the summit of the Andes where he had been heading to film his latest series for the production company. There was no information on whether anyone had survived.

Ethan heard voices in the hallway, and a moment later all three of his brothers were in the room. They all glanced over at Crissanne, and Hunter, who had lived in Malibu until recently and had met Crissanne a number of times, went to her and squeezed her shoulder.

"Don't worry. If anyone can find Mason it's Ethan," Hunter said.

"What can we do?" Nate asked.

"I don't know," Ethan said honestly, looking at his oldest brother. "I'm on hold with some officials in Peru. We are communicating but not as well as I'd like since my Spanish is more suited to ordering food or talking about legal matters."

"I've gotten pretty good lately," Derek said. Derek was a surgeon who had just married his best friend, Bianca Velasquez. She and her small son had been living in Spain until last year when she'd moved back to Cole's Hill.

"Do you mind?"

Derek gave him a hard look. "That's why we're here."

Ethan handed the landline phone to his brother, who took it out into the hallway. Hunter was chatting with Crissanne and distracting her from her own fears when Nate nodded to the hallway and Ethan followed him out there.

"What's going on? Dad said he'd seen you two in town last night and it might be a date," Nate said.

"Not now. We have bigger things—"

"No, you don't. You staring at your phone isn't going to make Mason safer or get information here quicker. What's going on?"

Ethan looked at his oldest brother and felt like a kid again. "I don't know. She showed up yesterday with her suitcase, saying things were over with her and Mason and she needed a place to stay."

"She's the one, isn't she? The one you are always visiting out in LA."

"I go to LA for business, not to see Crissanne. Though we usually have dinner, but that's the same thing I did with Hunter and Manu when they lived there." Manu Bennett was the brother of the famed astronaut Hemi Bennett, who was based at the local training center. Manu had been a defensive lineman in the NFL and until this year had been a special teams coach in California. But he'd recently moved to Cole's Hill to coach the high school team and to be closer to his brother and sister-in-law, Jessie, who was pregnant.

"She's not Hunt or Manu. I think you know that."

He shoved his hand through his hair and turned away from his brother before he punched him, though a fight might be what he needed right now. "Stop. I can't do this now. Whatever might have been possible before Mason disappeared is gone."

Nate nodded and then pulled him in for a quick hug. "Whatever happens, I got your back."

"I know and I appreciate it," Ethan said. "Depending on what happens I'll probably take the family jet to LA."

"Of course," Nate said.

Derek finished with the call and walked over to them. "So what they know is the plane went down after a Mayday call and they have dispatched rescue crews, but they aren't hopeful of finding any survivors."

"When will they know something?" Ethan asked, his heart sinking. A part of him still wanted to believe that his friend, who had always been so full of life and was sort of a superman, could survive the crash.

"They hope within twenty-four hours. They have our number and of course the production company's, but I reiterated that you needed to be informed at the same time. No sense getting information secondhand."

"Thanks, Derek," Ethan said. What was he going to tell Crissanne?

"No problem, bro," he said. "I'm bach-ing it this week while Bianca and Beni are in Spain visiting his grandparents. Want me to stay here? I can translate again." His brother had never really been into the bachelor lifestyle but now that he had a family he always referred to his time alone that way.

"Yeah, that'd be great," Ethan said.

Derek stopped smiling as he looked past Ethan's shoulder. He turned to see Crissanne standing there.

"The plane crashed, which we already knew, but Derek found out that the search-and-rescue crew has been dispatched and they are hoping to let us know something within twenty-four hours," he explained.

She nodded. "Okay."

Just that one little word. She looked lost, and he wanted his brothers gone so he could comfort her and talk to her. But he knew that he had to be careful there. He'd almost stepped over that line earlier.

"I guess all we can do is wait," she said.

"Yeah," Ethan agreed.

"Or you could get out of the house," Nate said. "It would be better if you went for a walk."

That was a good idea, Ethan thought. "Want to do it? My brothers will be here in case the Peruvians call back, and we both have our cells."

"Yes, let's do it," she said. "I'll go get my shoes on and be right back."

Ethan watched her run up the stairs from his spot in the hallway and then turned around to notice all three of his brothers watching him.

Hunter raised one eyebrow at him. "Is there—"

"No," Ethan said, brushing past his brothers and walking toward the front door. "Tell Crissanne I'm waiting outside for her."

He didn't hang around and risk an interrogation. He just stepped out into the hot August day. The sun was already high and temperatures were climbing. He threw his head back and looked up at the sky.

He wasn't ready to say goodbye to his best friend. He and Mason had a scuba trip planned for the Caribbean in September. And as much as he wanted Crissanne for his own, as much as he'd been tempted earlier, he knew he wanted his friend back more. He didn't want to lose this extra brother he'd found or the bond of friendship that was so strong between them.

* * *

Ethan lived in a gated community known as the Five Families. The houses were mansion-sized with well-landscaped lots. There were sidewalks and paved paths large enough to accommodate kids on their bikes and golf carts. There was a golf course, tennis courses and a country club with a sit-down restaurant and a bar, a pool with a snack bar, and several rooms that had private pool tables. She liked it. Ethan had spent the last ten minutes of their walk regaling her with all of those details in a nervous sort of rush.

"I feel it, too," she said at last, coming to a stop and waiting until he did. She had brought her Canon with her because she knew she needed to distract herself, and looking through her viewfinder always gave her distance from the problems in her life.

The problems that had led her to Cole's Hill and Ethan Caruthers. The problems that just kept getting worse.

"I can't stop thinking," he admitted wryly. "Guess I should have followed your advice and never started."

"I think that's impossible for both of us. It's just so odd. He broke up with me," Crissanne said, saying what was in her heart and in her mind to Ethan because he'd get it. "And if he came walking back in the front door this morning I wouldn't feel guilty—at least I don't think I would—but imagining him injured and waiting for help is confusing me."

Ethan nodded. He had his aviator-style Ray-Ban sunglasses on that made it nearly impossible to read his expression. She realized that she felt raw. Not just from the worry and fear about Mason, but from everything that had gone on between them the night before.

"Want to see the lake?" he asked.

"Sure. I didn't know there were many lakes in Texas," she said, pretty sure she'd read that the geology of the state meant that it didn't have many natural ones.

"There aren't. This one is man-made. When they built this subdivision they wanted it to be idyllic and sort of put in everything that we didn't have on the ranches," he said, resuming his pace. She fell into step beside him as Ethan again started talking nonstop about his family and this place.

She got it. Talking was how he distracted himself. When they were in college, she'd seen him debate with perfect strangers right before midterms and finals. He did it to keep himself from dwelling on whatever it was that worried him.

When they got close to the lake, she saw the beauty of the landscape and realized that she had an idea to get Ethan to stop talking and to distract herself.

"Pose for me," she said.

"What?"

"I need to take some pictures. I need to get my perspective back and I can only do that when I'm looking at the world through my lens. Will you let me take some photos of you?" she asked.

He turned to face her, crossing his arms over his chest, and she remembered how hard his muscles had been under her fingers last night. She swallowed as a rush of awareness went through her. But no guilt.

Just curiosity.

She was upset about Mason, so it was especially surprising that she didn't feel guilty about Ethan.

She took the lens cap off, lifted her camera and took a few photos just to check the light. Even if he didn't pose, she needed this. She wanted to see the land and find her center.

"I didn't say yes," he said, but his lips had quirked as soon as she lifted her camera.

"You didn't say no."

He turned away from her and she caught her breath. His broad shoulders tapered to a lean waist, and his faded jeans, the same ones he'd had on last night, hugged the curves of his butt and his lean thighs. So it hadn't just been tequila and moonlight. It had been Ethan.

She'd sort of suspected that, but it was easy in the clear light of day to pretend that it was something else. Anything else.

Especially when he seemed so nervous around her today.

It was impossible not to see it and feel it as they'd waited tensely for the production company to call with more details. And then there was this walk, where he'd talked about everything but what was between the two of them.

And she got it. Men didn't like to talk. How many times had Mason told her that? But Ethan was a talker...well, sort of.

"I like your boots," she said. He had on a Western-cut pair today. They were in good shape but she could tell they were worn in. They had probably gotten to that comfortable stage.

She moved around to see the different effects of the light and realized that looking through the lens was for her what talking about this place was for him.

"Tell me about the lake," she said.

He glanced at her and she snapped a couple of quick photos. Her camera could capture an unguarded expression that would be too quick for her eye, and she couldn't wait to examine the photos later.

"It was debated for three years before they finally got around to digging it out, according to my papaw. He said that there was some discussion of whether it should be one mixed-use lake or two different lakes—one for swimming and small watercraft and the other for fishing."

He continued to tell her the story as she moved around taking pictures. For a short time, she almost forgot that the man they had in common was missing. But she knew if she wanted to find her own peace with Mason and Ethan, she needed to ensure that she didn't ruin the men's friendship.

"Tell me about how you and Mason became friends," she said.

Surprised, he turned to face her, but she was hidden behind the camera. So many people used the digital display when they took pictures nowadays.

"Why aren't you looking at the screen?" he asked.

"I like the way the world looks when I'm shooting," she said, dropping the camera from her face and looking over at him with a smile.

She was so much more relaxed with the camera in her hands. She seemed like she was breathing more easily now that they were out of the house. It was the same for him. He'd felt the walls closing in even before his brothers had arrived.

"You know how you said that I was lucky to have my brothers?" he asked her.

"Yes. I still think that," she said.

"I do, too. The best part about family is that you don't have to ask for them to be there," he said, not realizing how his words might sound to her until he saw the wistful expression on her face.

"That must be nice."

"It is. It can be a pain in the ass as well. That's sort of how Mason and I became friends. By the time I went to college, Derek had been away for a few years and Nate had just gone to College Station, but I was determined to go to Harvard. So I studied and worked my ass off to get there. My parents, who are very supportive, were determined to make sure that I didn't feel lonely up in Cambridge. So they all went up there with me."

"That doesn't sound so bad," she said.

"I don't mean just my parents. My brothers all came, even Hunter, who was going to college in Northern California," he said. "I had arranged to do a house share. My dad was checking out the locks and my mom was in the kitchen cooking casseroles I could heat up for the week and my brothers were setting up stuff…it was just, I'd picked Cambridge because I had gotten sick of being a Caruthers in Cole's Hill. Everyone knows everything about you here, and I realized that no matter where I went they'd be there."

"You carry them with you," she said. Just like she carried that image in her head of the parents she wished she'd known. She had no idea what they looked like. In her teenage years, she'd spent hours staring at herself in the mirror wondering if she had her mom's eyes or her father's coloring. Finally she'd cut a picture out of a magazine and put it in a cheap plastic frame that one of the other kids at the foster home had thrown out and decided the people in the photo were her parents.

She hadn't thought of that in years. If Mason didn't come back from Peru, she'd really be all alone.

It wasn't like she'd made any other close bonds in the last ten years. There was Ethan and Mason, and to a certain extent Abby in San Francisco, but that was it.

"I do," he said. "That's partly why I ended up back here. Didn't make sense to be out there in the great big world, you know?"

She nodded. "So how did you meet Mason?"

"He didn't have any family, as you know, and all the stuff about my family that made me crazy, he loved. When I got back to the house share from running an errand, he was sitting in the kitchen taking notes as my mom told him how to make tuna casserole."

That made Crissanne laugh. "Oh my God. That's his only dinner dish."

Ethan smiled, too. "He never forgets anything."

"He doesn't," she said. "God, I hope he's okay."

"Me, too," he admitted. "We're supposed to go on vacation in September. Just a week of scuba diving."

"He hadn't mentioned it," she said.

"He didn't?"

"No," she said. "We haven't been in the same room for more than an hour in a long time."

Ethan hadn't realized that. She had said things were over, but he hadn't believed it. Had Mason been avoiding Crissanne?

"I'm sorry."

"You know what, Eth, that was a big part of what pushed me to force him into a relationship discussion. I want a family. I've never had one of my own and we've been together for a long time… so I just waited at home. I turned down a job and waited for him. I had to know."

Ethan moved closer to her.

"What did you have to know?"

"Why he was avoiding me," she said. "And he

finally said he liked us the way we had been. The fun stuff. He wasn't ready for a family."

"But you were."

"Yup, and he said that he didn't see himself that way. Not ever."

That sucked. Big-time. For both of them. "I'm sorry."

"Me, too. We fought and then he left and I came here and now his plane has crashed…" She made a broken sound. "The last words I said to him weren't very nice. I have spent the better part of the last twelve years with him and I was just… a bitch."

"No," he said. "I don't know what you said, but I know you weren't a bitch. And I do know one thing about Mason. When things get too close and he needs space, he forces the situation to make the other person react. He did that to me when I was dithering about staying in LA or coming back here."

"Did he?"

"Yes," Ethan said. "Don't feel bad about what you said. Mason knows how you really feel about him. And he's going to be found and you'll have a chance to talk to him again. Soon."

Five

Ethan had never spent a longer day than this one. His brothers had gone home since they weren't expecting any news till tomorrow. Apparently there was a weather system keeping the rescuers from reaching the wreckage. So no news.

Crissanne had gone to her room when they'd returned, and he hadn't seen her in the last eight hours. He was restless, and that was never good. He thought about leaving the house and heading to the Bull Pen, where he'd be sure to find some outlet for the energy inside him. He could ride the mechanical bull or even find one of his frenemies from high school to fight with in the parking lot. But Ethan liked to think he was beyond that.

He heard Bart out by the pool and went outside. The other man was talking to Crissanne.

Ethan stayed where he was in the shadows.

"If you don't check the balances every day they could change. The sun sometimes causes certain ones to burn up quicker than others."

"That sounds a lot like science to me," Crissanne said as she took photos of the pool. "I've never been one to understand that."

Bart laughed. "Chemistry is my thing. Well, it used to be my downfall, but Ethan helped me find a better way to channel my interests."

"He's good about that," Crissanne said. "He always sees the best in everyone."

Ethan knew he needed to leave or announce himself, but he was interested to hear how Crissanne really saw him and was tempted to stay. His phone pinged, and he glanced at the screen.

Crissanne and Bart both turned toward the noise.

"The production company has news and wants to video chat with us. Do you want to do it out here or in my office?" he asked.

She had gone completely white when he said that they had news. In fact he felt the same way.

Good news could have been texted. There was no reason why they couldn't have said *he's alive*.

"Inside." Crissanne's voice was low, gravelly and raw.

He reached for her hand, and she took his. Her grip was tight, as if he were her lifeline to whatever was coming next.

"Let's go."

The hallway to his office just off the foyer was short, but it felt like it took forever to get there. He entered the bookshelf-lined room that his mom had helped him decorate. That had been their thing when he'd been growing up. Books. When they'd traveled, she'd taken him to secondhand shops all over Texas and the country, and they'd collected old leather-bound volumes.

He knew he should be thinking about Mason, about the call. Instead he was trying to comfort himself with thoughts of his mom and their collecting.

"I'm scared."

Crissanne's voice brought him back to the moment. He could deal with his own emotions later; right now he needed to help her through this. She was looking to him to be the one to stay strong, and he would.

Of course he would.

He set his iPad on a console table on one side of

the room, and he and Crissanne sat on the leather love seat right across from it.

"Ready?"

She nodded.

He engaged the video call and then sat down next to her. She wrapped her arm through his and hugged it to her chest. He looked down at her, the girl with no family who had given twelve years of her life to a man who then said he didn't want to start one with her, and his heart broke a little bit. But he knew that whatever had happened at the end between her and Mason, there had been love there, and friendship.

And he didn't want to see her lose everything.

The call connected and the screen was clear.

"Uh…thanks for doing this on video. I'm Cam Jones," the man at the production company said.

"Cam, you have news for us?" Ethan asked, getting right to the point.

"I do. There's no easy way to say this. The rescuers got to the wreckage and they didn't find Mason. There was a fire after the plane crashed, and no bodies were recovered."

Crissanne started to cry softly next to him.

Ethan pulled his arm free of hers and wrapped it around her shoulder. He didn't want to believe what Cam was telling them. It was unfathomable that Mason would die in a plane crash.

"Are you sure he's dead?"

Cam nodded. "You know Mason has skills, so we told the rescuers to search the surrounding area of the crash, and nothing…no one was found. Mason Murray is dead."

The words echoed in Ethan's mind. He knew Cam was still talking, but he turned to look at Crissanne, who was sobbing as she buried her face in his chest. All he could do was hold her.

He held his best friend's ex-girlfriend and wondered how he was going to get through this without Mason to talk sense to him. Mason, who'd always been the one to get that even though to the world Ethan seemed to have all his shit together, he still was treading water.

Every. Damned. Day.

And now he had to help Crissanne.

He would focus on her. That would have to be enough to get him through this. Until she was okay, he'd just keep his own grief bottled up.

But he'd lost a brother today. He'd lost someone he wasn't ready to let go of, and he had no idea how he was going to cope.

"Will you be coming to LA?" Cam asked.

"I'll get back to you later today. But yes, we will be there."

The video call disconnected and he just held Crissanne. It was what he'd always wanted. To have a clear shot at this woman. But now it was all wrong. He'd never wanted to have her at the cost of Mason. For a moment last night, it had almost seemed possible, but then he knew the things he craved the most were always the ones that were just out of his reach.

Crissanne had been alone before. And she and Mason had broken up. So she wasn't sure why she couldn't stop crying.

Ethan was being very sweet. He'd told her to just sit in the sun while his housekeeper packed her bags. Bart had disappeared into the pool house and she sat there, trying to make sense of it all.

Mason gone.

It didn't seem real to her. How had that happened?

The sense of loss she felt was so strong that she just kept crying. Honestly, she'd had no idea she could cry that much. The tears just fell, and when she'd calm down and be able to stop for a moment, they'd just start right back up again.

She wanted Mason back. She didn't want him back in her life as her boyfriend. That had been over long before this breakup. But she wanted her friend back. He was the only person she had shared so much with over the last twelve years.

And even those memories weren't as full as

they could have been. In their last argument, he'd said they were strangers, more like casual friends who slept together when it was convenient for both of them. Not a real couple. But she hadn't understood until this moment. As their life together flashed before her eyes, she realized that most of it was her waiting for him and getting back to him. Not actually spending time with him. She finally got what Mason was saying. Damn him for going to extremes to prove his point.

"You were right," she said out loud. "You win. Come back and I'll tell you to your face."

But he wasn't coming back. He was gone. Lost to her forever like the parents she'd never known. And her weary heart shrank even further in her chest. How many times did she have to see the same message before it sank in?

She drew her knees to her chest on the lounge chair and put her forehead against them. She had always believed deep inside that she was meant for something more. That she'd grow up and make the family she never had. But the truth was she'd never learned to bond with anyone. How was she going to have a family when she couldn't connect?

"Crissy?"

She glanced over at Ethan. Sweet Ethan, who was helping her through something that was horrible for him, too. He always put her first and she just used him…

"Yes."

"Whatever it is that's going through your mind, stop it," he said.

"What?"

"I can see it on your face. The guilt and the loneliness and the sadness, all of it. And the truth is you are entitled to all of those feelings, but you aren't responsible in any way for what happened."

"I know that," she said, but realized that Ethan had nailed it. That was what she was afraid of. "But I told him I never wanted to see him again. Eth, I said that to him. I walked away muttering that it would be better if he were dead."

"You didn't mean it."

"I know that. But I said it. I put that out in the universe."

He came over to her, sat down on the end of her lounge chair and put his hand on her calf.

She looked up and their gazes met, his gray-green eyes so intent and serious. "You're human. We all get mad and say things we don't mean. It happens. And he'd broken up with you. Don't judge yourself by that one moment. You didn't do anything to Mason's plane. You didn't force him to go."

No, she hadn't. And she wouldn't have been

able to live with him after what they'd said. Because there was more to the fight than she could share with Ethan. "I wanted him to stay. I didn't want him to take this trip, which is what started our fight."

"Which makes everything that much harder to deal with," Ethan said. "I think he would have done anything to get back to you."

Crissanne nodded. But she knew that wasn't true. And she was still too close to the heartbreak he'd given her to be able to remember just his good parts. That was what Ethan was trying to make her do: remember the best of Mason. "At least he died doing what he loved."

"Yes. He did. He loved going out on his adventures and filming them. He wouldn't have wanted to live any other way," Ethan said.

"He said as much to me when we fought. His life wasn't meant for suburbia."

Ethan nodded. "He told me one time that he'd learned to survive on his own because he knew no one was there for him. He liked being in the wilderness because there was no illusion that anyone was looking out for him. He knew it was just him and nature. And nature didn't allow sentimentality."

Crissanne had to smile at that. "That's so Mason. I'm sure he followed it with his usual mantra…if you depend on yourself you won't be let down."

"He did. And I can only say I'm sure he wasn't," Ethan said.

But Crissanne knew that she was. Of course she'd depended on herself, but she'd always wanted more. She'd always expected to have more and now she was alone. Truly alone again. And though Ethan had been lovely, she couldn't come back to his town, his life, his house after this.

It was time to start living the way she'd always pretended she wasn't going to, by depending on herself.

But as Ethan got to his feet and offered her his hand, she realized just how hard it was going to be to walk away from him.

Ethan wanted to get in his Ferrari and just drive. Go out on the old FM road that went out of town and put the pedal down. Go as fast as he could for as long as he could, scream out his grief and frustration about the ending of Mason's life, but he couldn't.

Instead he'd driven them sedately through town to the private airport that had become bigger and busier since the NASA training facility opened. When they got there, he'd busied himself with talking to the pilot and copilot and texting his assistant.

In fact, he had a list of things that needed to be taken care of. He'd put Crissanne at the top, but he knew he had to pull back and distance himself. He had to give her room to grieve. He had cases he had to refer to other attorneys in his practice. He had to make sure that the oil rights he'd been negotiating for the Rockin' C were taken care of. Hunter had taken care of letting his staff know that Ethan would be staying at his house in Malibu for a few days.

Now he was ready to go, but he paused to take in Crissanne. She stood there on the tarmac looking so damned beautiful that it took his breath away. She had on a pair of large-framed sunglasses that covered half of her face and her blond hair blew in the wind. She'd put on a pair of black skinny jeans that showcased her long legs and a short-sleeved T-shirt.

She looked like she was coping, but he saw her surreptitiously wipe away a tear just then. She was going to be grieving and coming to terms with Mason's loss for a long time.

She looked like…she looked like everything he'd ever wanted, but she was still out of reach.

He had just finished filing the paperwork, paying for the fuel and making sure they were set to go. He walked out of the small airport office toward the waiting G6.

"All set," he said. "I wasn't sure if you'd want to stay with me at Hunter's house or at your place…"

"It's not my place. I already moved out. If you don't mind, I'd like to stay with you."

"That's why I offered," he said.

He cupped her elbow and led her to the stairs up to the plane. When they got inside, she took a seat on one of the large leather chairs.

"Why does your family have a private plane?"

"Why not, right?" Ethan asked.

"I guess, but it doesn't strike me as something you'd all need," she said.

"Well…are you sure you want to talk about this?" he asked.

"Yes. I need to talk about something or I'm going to go crazy just thinking about Mason and what could have been."

What could have been. The words echoed in his mind and he shoved them away.

"Well, as you know, Hunter was accused of a crime he didn't commit," Ethan said. "So while he was playing for the NFL he flew mainly on private jets to avoid possible confrontations. It started the first time he was coming home one year for Thanksgiving and flew commercial. Some people on the plane thought he was guilty and weren't shy about expressing their opinions. They made the flight hell for him, and my father came to me and said we don't fly commercial anymore. So we bought the plane and now we all use it."

Ethan didn't like to talk about that long period of time when Hunter had been living under a cloud of suspicion. In college, a female classmate had died under mysterious circumstances and Hunter and a classmate had been suspects in the investigation. But the Carutherses had all stood by Hunter because the boy who loved God, football and his girlfriend would never have committed a crime like that. But to the outside world, Hunter had looked like a privileged boy who thought that rules didn't apply to him.

"I'm glad we did. It is a nice asset for us to have," he continued, when Crissanne didn't say anything.

"I'm glad, too. I can't believe people. Hunter wasn't even arrested for that crime," Crissanne said. She knew the details because of their years of friendship.

"True. But you know how it is with social media and the court of public opinion," Ethan said. "On the subject of the public, the production company asked me to write a statement for them to release from Mason's family and friends."

"They did?"

"Yes. They were going to ask you, but Cam said he didn't think you'd be in the right frame of mind to write it. He was worried that it would be overwhelming for you."

"Does he know that Mason broke up with me?"

Ethan had no idea. "He said it because of how upset you were by the news on our video call."

She bit her lower lip. "I don't want to be dishonest, but if people are going to treat me like I'm Mason's girlfriend, what am I going to do?"

"Just be honest," Ethan said. "Do what you feel comfortable with."

The pilot leaned his head through the cockpit door and advised them to put their seat belts on and get ready for takeoff. Ethan sat down across the aisle from Crissanne and put on his seat belt.

She reached out and touched his arm.

"Thank you."

He smiled over at her. She still looked so sad that his heart ached, and he knew he would do everything in his power to make her smile again. He would put all of his resources behind helping her through this.

"That's what friends do," he said.

"You're more than a friend, Ethan. And this means more to me than I can say," she admitted. "I'm used to doing things on my own and just getting through it."

He took her hand in his, laced their fingers together and ignored the tingle that continued to run through him from when he first touched her arm. She needed him.

And that was really all that mattered right now.

Six

After three weeks in Los Angeles, she felt like she was in a fog. She had since they'd first landed here and she'd felt the sun on her face. She'd felt that way the entire time they'd stayed at Ethan's brother's oceanfront house in Malibu, as they handled all kinds of questions and paperwork.

Each day Ethan left her a note with the house-keeper letting her know where he was and what he was doing. He had paid for another team to go to Peru and search for Mason. Today, he'd asked her to come downtown to his firm's LA office. So that was how she found herself standing in the lobby of a high-rise building, wearing her one decent-looking dress and heels. Because she knew that no matter how West Coast casual she was, his law firm wasn't.

When she took the elevator up to the third floor, the receptionist gave her a bottle of sparkling water and directed her to a conference room that overlooked the Fashion District. She had her camera with her and intended to spend some time walking around there when she was done. She hadn't been able to make videos or write at all since the news of Mason's death had reached them, but she'd taken so many pictures and had been publishing them on her blog instead. Just faces of people she met on the beach each day as she walked and searched for answers that were still out of reach.

The door opened and she turned around, feeling a piece of her hair slip from the clip she had it pulled back in. Ethan was wearing nicely tailored suit pants but had taken off his jacket. His hair was mussed. He slipped his phone into his pocket as he walked toward her.

"Sorry to make you come all the way down here. Did you drive?" he asked. He'd also left a car and driver for her use.

"No," she said. "I hate LA traffic so I asked

Peter to drive me. I told him I'd catch a ride back with you."

"I might be working late," he said.

Of course he was. He'd been avoiding being alone with her.

"I'm planning to go down to the Fashion District to get some photos for my blog, so I'm not in a hurry."

"Well, okay then. I've had a report from the team we sent," Ethan said, coming farther into the room and holding out a chair at the table for her.

They sat down and Ethan pulled the tablet that had been on the table closer to him. She watched his hands moving on the tablet as he entered the pass code. For a brief moment, she flashed to what those hands could do to her. She had spent a lot of time on her walks on the beach thinking of that one night they'd had before everything had gone so crazy.

"Okay. Did they find anything? Any signs that he might still be alive?" she asked.

He pulled up a file. An image of the burned fuselage of the plane flashed on the screen. He swiped, and the next photo showed six body bags.

Horrified, she turned away. This was it.

It was real. Mason was dead. He was gone.

Really gone, and there was nothing that could bring him back.

She hadn't realized she was crying until Ethan handed her a handkerchief. She turned away. It was funny how she had been able to reach for him before, but not any longer. The more time they spent together the more distance had grown between them.

She felt the sting of tears, but she'd already known that Mason was gone. It wasn't the sweeping grief it had been the first time. She sighed and reached for the tablet for a closer look at the photo.

"I hate that he died like that," she said at last.

"Me, too," Ethan said. His voice was the same monotone it had been since they'd heard the news.

She didn't think he was fully processing his grief, but because he was always working or taking a call about work she'd had no chance to talk to him about that.

"Are we friends?" she asked him.

"What?"

He turned to look at her, and for a moment she caught a glimpse of the sorrow in his eyes before he masked it with his normal calm expression.

"Are we friends?" she asked again, turning the swivel chair to face him and then putting her hands on the arms of his chair and pivoting it until they were face-to-face. He had to move his legs to either side of hers to ensure they could both sit comfortably.

"Yes. Why do you think we aren't?"

She put her hand on his knee, and he jerked his leg from under her touch. "Since we've been here you've been running away from me. We haven't talked about anything that's important, and I'm sick of your damned notes from the housekeeper. Are you just saying we're friends so that I won't be alone?"

He shook his head.

"What is it? I can't keep doing this. I know that I, out of everyone, should be used to going solo but this isn't what I expect when I'm with you."

"I know," he said, taking her hand in his and turning it over. He started rubbing his thumb over her palm, which caused a warm sensation throughout her body.

"Okay, so what's going on?"

"I…I…" He dropped her hand and got up, walking to the plate glass windows that looked down on the street.

She waited for him to see what it was he would say, but instead he just put his head against the glass. He looked like she felt inside. So alone.

She got up and went over to him, but was afraid to reach out in case he pushed her away again.

"I can't let out even a moment of what I'm feeling," he said at last, his voice so soft it was barely a gravelly thread. "If I do, I'm not sure I'll be able to control it."

Ethan had been doing his level best to remind himself that Crissanne was vulnerable now. More than she had been when she'd shown up on his doorstep. He wanted to think that it had meant something—her appearing like that—but a part of him suspected it had to be that she'd wanted to make Mason jealous.

Mason.

Ethan had been very careful not to let himself dwell on his friend's death. His best friend. Mason was the one who had truly known him best. Ethan was close with his brothers, but they all had their own lives and careers. It was Mason he called in the middle of the night when he was fighting his own demons, and Mason had always reached out to him when he was in the middle of something he didn't know how to control.

Which was why the breakup with Crissanne had taken him by surprise.

Mason had been quiet about it.

And Ethan would never have the chance to talk to his friend now. He missed him. He could admit that around 2:00 a.m. when he was sitting in his bed not sleeping, but not now. It was the middle of the afternoon in his office building. He had to keep his shit together.

Crissanne put her hand on his shoulder. A comforting gesture to be sure, but at the same time it sent a tingle down his back that he couldn't ignore. He needed something mindless. He wanted sex with a stranger but that wasn't happening. Even if Crissanne weren't staying at Hunter's house with him, she was the only one turning him on these days.

She was so close her body heat was surrounding him, and when he glanced into the plate glass window he saw her reflection. Saw the way she was watching him. And then her fingers moved against his shoulder. He had left his suit jacket in his office, so it was just the two thin layers of his oxford shirt and the T-shirt he had on underneath keeping her from touching his skin.

His blood seemed to flow more heavily through his body and he turned to her, head down, intent on walking away. But she was close, and their foreheads bumped. He felt the startled exhalation of her breath against his lips and then he felt her lips against his.

He grabbed her waist and drew her closer to him, more fully into contact with him, and he knew he wasn't going to let go. Not this time. Not until he was buried between her legs and doing what he should have done that night. That night before—

"Say no and leave," he said, his voice so low and gruff that he hated it. All the trappings of the civilized man he'd learned to be were falling away. "Because if you don't I'm going to lock the conference room door and have you right here on this table."

She chewed her lower lip between her teeth and then nodded. She dropped her hand from his shoulder and turned away from him.

Fuck. He'd known he couldn't let his guard down. That he was throwing away something with Crissanne that had always been hard for him to process and understand. But then she stopped at the door. Instead of opening it, she turned the lock on the handle and then leaned back against it.

"I'm not leaving," she said.

Hell, yeah.

He didn't think anymore. Thinking hadn't done a damned thing except make him hyperaware of how little control he had over any part of his life.

Instead he walked across the room toward her and she stayed right where she was. Watching him with those eyes of hers. He put one hand on the door behind her head and the other on her waist. She tipped her head back as he lowered his toward her, but he didn't want to kiss her again. He wanted to taste that long length of her neck.

He sucked at the skin there. She smelled of strawberries and the ocean. Her skin was tanned and smooth. He wanted to be a gentleman and take his time, but he'd waited a lifetime for her and he knew that wasn't going to happen.

He lifted her off her feet as he turned his head, plunging his tongue deep into her mouth. She wrapped her thighs around his hips and held his face in his hands, angling her head for a deeper kiss as she rubbed her center against him.

He pushed his hand up under her skirt, feeling the coolness of her bare thigh, and then sliding it higher to her butt. He slipped his hand underneath the fabric of her panties and then cupped one cheek in his hand, running his finger along the crack.

She shifted again, pulling her mouth from his and whispering something he couldn't understand. He was beyond listening or thinking. He was focused on her. On having her.

With one hand, he lowered his zipper and shoved his pants and underwear out of the way so that his dick was free. She reached down, brushing his hands aside as she stroked him, her fist wrapping around him and her finger rubbing over the tip of him with each stroke.

He set her on her feet, and she hopped from one foot to the other as she pushed her panties down her legs and then stepped out of them. She glanced up at him and he knew he should say something. Make this seem like it was about more than sex and forgetting, but he couldn't.

Instead, he put his hand on her waist and stepped closer to her. The wall was at her back, and Ethan was pressed along the front of her body. The cloth of her skirt rubbed over his erection and he pulled his hips back, realizing he needed protection.

"Dammit. I don't have a condom."

"It's okay. I'm on the pill," she said.

Ethan lifted his hand, rubbing it over the line of her jaw, and she shivered. She realized she wanted to touch him. She didn't want to settle for half measures, because this might be the only time he dropped his guard enough. She felt his thigh between her legs and shuddered as he cupped her butt with his hand and drew her forward. She undid the buttons on his shirt, but found he was wearing a T-shirt underneath it.

Frustrated, she tugged the shirt up his chest until the hem was right underneath his armpits. Then she bit her lower lip as she drew her fingers over his bare chest and abdomen. His muscles were hard; she knew that from that long-ago night that she'd touched him. But now she felt his heat and realized how much she'd forgotten as she skimmed her fingers over his chest. There was that light dusting of hair that tapered down to his groin and she caressed it, following the line as he continued to fondle her backside.

She was creamy and wet for him, and drawing this out was out of the question. She reached between them and stroked her hand down the length of his shaft, pulling him forward between her legs, rubbing the tip of his dick against herself. She bit her own lip and closed her eyes, letting her head fall back as sensations ran through her.

But it wasn't enough. She wanted him inside her. She needed him deeply filling her, and she wanted it now.

She shifted on his thigh, moving her hips forward and pushing his erection down until he was poised at the entrance of her body. His hands tightened on her ass, and he bit the point where her neck and shoulder met as he drew back his hips and then drove them forward.

She groaned as he filled her, digging her nails into his lean hips and holding on tight.

He muttered her name. "You feel so good."

She nodded. She couldn't think, could only feel. She tightened herself around him, and he groaned against her neck as he pulled out and then plunged back into her again.

She smiled as she rotated her hips to adjust to him inside her. She wanted him deep, filling her completely.

He tightened his hands on her backside as he continued driving himself up and into her, and suddenly everything inside her felt on edge. She was close to her orgasm. He sucked hard on her neck and she threw her head back, calling his name as she came. He tightened his hold on her, driving into her hard and deep until she felt him shudder in her arms and he emptied himself inside her.

She closed her eyes, resting her head on his shoulder as he held her. Her body kept tightening around him and his breath sawed in and out of his mouth. He moved his arms up her back to hold her and she just breathed deeply, realizing it had been too long since she'd had sex.

That had to be the reason why she was holding on to him so tightly and why she felt like crying. She'd been alone for so long, and having him inside her and his arms around her made her realize what it was she wanted in her life.

She needed more of this. More of him. And it had nothing to do with Mason's death. It had to do with Ethan, and what she'd been hiding from herself for too long. She wanted what Ethan had to offer. This quiet intensity.

He shifted, pulling out of her, and he set her on her feet, stepping away. "Uh, I didn't think this through at all. There is a restroom down the hall."

"Ethan?"

"Hmm?"

"Are we okay?" she asked. Because he wasn't looking at her. Hadn't looked at her since he'd shifted out of her body.

He'd turned his back to her, and when he turned back around, his T-shirt was tucked into his pants and his zipper was up. He was doing the buttons up on his shirt, and she felt like the impact of the sex had been stronger for her than for him. Maybe he'd just needed to come and then he could breathe again.

"Yeah. We are," he said. But that flat note was back in his voice again.

She almost turned away. Almost let him force them back to the détente they'd been living in for the last three weeks. But instead she walked over to him, stumbling over her discarded panties. When she glanced up, she caught his unguarded expression.

He wasn't as aloof as he was trying to be.

"Good. Because I'm done with the distance between us. I came to you before Mason's plane crashed because my life was at a crossroads and I thought…I thought I knew what I wanted. Mason's death has made me realize that life is short. None of us is guaranteed a long life and I'm tired of always waiting…"

She stepped back. "I'm not waiting anymore, Ethan. I want more than friendship with you, and I think you want something more from me, too."

He rubbed his hand over his chest and looked at her. For the first time she saw the pain and hope and guilt in his eyes, and she knew that he wanted more than they'd been sharing lately.

"Let's go home. Let's go back to Cole's Hill and figure out if this is just a reaction or something solid," he finally said.

Seven

It had been all well and good to say he wanted to go home, but there was still Mason's memorial to get through. Meanwhile, Crissanne had moved into his bedroom. Not that she took up that much space, but she had a big presence. Everywhere he looked, there were signs of her. Right now, he was in the big en suite bathroom with the double sinks. He didn't even have to turn his head to see her perfume bottle and makeup brushes on the counter. She was in the bedroom singing off-key to Liam Gallagher's "For What It's Worth."

He took a break from doing his black tie in

a Windsor knot and put his hands on the sink counter. If there was a song that was more about Mason he'd never heard it. The first one to fly... he'd been that one; he'd always gone above and beyond. He had a temper and he had been brutal in his honesty, and it was only now that he was gone that Ethan could admit even to himself that Mason had been the one to see through his facade.

Fuck.

He'd always been able to see through it. Even when they'd been at school the first year and Ethan was trying to mask the fact that he was using drugs to stay up late and get in all the studying he needed to. Trying to hide that he'd gone beyond just using drugs to study and had started becoming addicted.

But he hadn't fooled Mason.

He saw it and didn't try anything like counseling or talking to him. He had punched Ethan hard in the jaw. He'd been pissed as hell and punched him back, but Mason hadn't stopped. They'd beat the shit out of each other that night and when it was over, Mason explained that he'd never had what Ethan had. No parents who cared or brothers who dropped by. Ethan was a damned lucky fuck, so he needed to stop screwing up his life.

That was it.

Mason had never said another word and Ethan

had stopped using. It had been hard, but he always remembered looking into Mason's green eyes in that bruised and bloodied face and hearing the longing in his friend's voice. It had gotten through to him in a way nothing else had been able to.

"Damn, I miss you, brother," he said. The words were drawn out of him and he felt—oh, hell, no, he wasn't going to cry.

He had been strong until this point and he wasn't about to give in now. He had to stay strong. He pushed the heels of his hands into his eye sockets and held them there so tightly he saw stars, breathing in through his nostrils until he felt that need pass. He dropped his hands, cleared his throat and went back to work on his tie.

He needed to do it for himself and for Crissanne, who was coming to be more than he'd expected her to be. He knew a part of him wanted her because she was pretty, with those long legs and her easy smile. Her offbeat sense of humor had caught him off guard more than once. But getting to know the real woman was making him fall for her. Legitimately fall for her, not for the illusion of wanting a girl who was off-limits.

This was different.

She was different.

And he wanted to be different, too.

But he'd always been better on paper than in

real life. The third son of a prominent ranching family. The smart lawyer who was good in court. The man who never left any broken hearts because he'd never let himself really care.

He heard her in the doorway and looked over to see her standing there, dressed all in black. The sheath dress hugged her curves and ended just above the knee. She had her hair pulled up and she wore a pair of pearl earrings that he knew Mason had given her. He'd been with him when he'd purchased them.

"You okay?" she asked, but she stayed where she was.

"Yeah. Today is going to be a tough one," he admitted.

She nodded. "It is. But it will be good to say goodbye to him. Now that we know he isn't coming back."

"Did you think he might have been?" Ethan asked.

She shrugged. "Obviously I thought I'd run into him again. You and he are friends and if I stayed with you…"

It was there again, that thought that he'd been careful not to allow to fully form before. "And you were with me to make him jealous?"

She shook her head.

"It wasn't that at all. It was more about you

than about Mason. I came to you because when I thought of being alone in the world, and about the one person I knew I could count on, it was you, Ethan."

He finished up his tie and then turned his back to her to undo his trousers and tuck his shirt in. The action was more to give himself time and distance than because he was bashful. He wanted to believe that he hadn't betrayed Mason when he'd kissed Crissanne the first time. Or when he'd taken her in his office. But a part of him couldn't get square with the idea.

He felt her hand on the center of his back and it startled him. As he stood stock-still, she said, "I never meant to be something else you had to regret."

Did she see him that way?

"I don't," he said, turning to face her. She had put on makeup that changed the shape of her eyes. She still looked like herself, but so different from the girl she usually was. The black liner made her eyes look wider and more exotic, but the truth that stared at him from them was the same. She always watched him like she was afraid of something.

The memorial service was held at a funeral home in Malibu. When Crissanne entered with Ethan she was surprised to see his entire family waiting there. His dad came over and gave her a hug, his weathered face full of concern. Ethan's brothers and sisters-in-law were there, too. Two little kids sat quietly in one corner reading a book.

The little girl had red hair that was up in pigtails and wore a black dress that had a horse embroidered on the skirt. The little boy wore a tiny black suit with a bow tie. Both of them couldn't have been more than three or four years old, but they were well behaved and clearly shared a close friendship.

"I hope it's okay that we brought the kids," Kinley Caruthers said as she came over to her. Crissanne knew all of Ethan's sisters-in-law as he'd sent her pictures after each of the weddings. Kinley was married to Ethan's oldest brother, Nate. She and Nate had apparently had a hot Vegas weekend that had resulted in a child. But Nate hadn't found out about his daughter until last year.

"Of course. Thank you for coming," Crissanne said. "I'm surprised at how well behaved they are."

"Benito's father died last year," Ethan's other sister-in-law Bianca said, coming over to them. The former supermodel had married a Formula One driver but he had died in a plane crash. She'd come home to Cole's Hill, where she and Derek Caruthers had rekindled their friendship and that had led to love.

Bianca wrapped her arm around Crissanne's shoulder and gave her a quick hug. "It's sad to say it, but he knows how to behave at a funeral."

It was sad. "Where are you all staying?"

"We are going to be at Hunter's tonight," Kinley said. "There wasn't time to get over there this morning."

"When did you decide to come?" Crissanne asked. Ethan hadn't mentioned to her that his family was going to be at the memorial service.

"I don't think there was a discussion. More like Nate saying let's go," Kinley said. "That man tends to take his big-brother role seriously."

"Derek had to finish surgery before we could leave," Bianca explained. "Hunter and Ferrin were already at the airport."

More people started to file in and Crissanne moved away from the Caruthers family as she recognized the people from the production company and past film shoots that Mason had been on. She talked to them for a few minutes, and then the funeral director came to find her and asked her if she wanted to have a few minutes alone before the service started.

She wasn't sure.

In the end, she nodded because the reception room was getting too full of people she really didn't know. She followed him into a room that was set up like a church. In the spot where a casket would have been if they had the body, there was an easel with a portrait of Mason on it. She walked away from the man and moved toward the front of the room and the picture.

It was one she'd taken. She'd been expecting to see it, but with the flowers around it and the pressure of just being here, suddenly she missed him keenly.

She reached out to touch his face. She remembered the exact day she'd taken the photo. They'd been out on his catamaran sailing between Dana Point and Catalina. He'd been trying to teach her how to sail, but the sun had felt too good on her skin and she'd just lounged around, letting him do all the work, taking photos with her waterproof camera.

He'd been in his element.

That day she'd seen what he looked like when he was in love. Maybe that was when she had first realized that she was competing with nature and she'd never win when it came to Mason.

The door opened behind her and she glanced around to see Ethan standing there. "I hope you don't mind my joining you."

"Of course not. You need to say your goodbyes privately, too," she said.

"I do," Ethan admitted. "It's hard for me to deal with emotion."

"I know," she said quietly. "I think that's one thing I liked about you and Mason together. He'd lose his temper or jump up and scale a rock face and you'd be sitting there quietly weighing the pros and cons or talking him down from the edge."

Ethan shook his head. "Mason always called me his safety net."

"You were," she agreed. That sounded like Mason. Like what he'd said to her as he'd walked away. She was his chance at normal. But that normal wasn't in the cards for him.

"I was surprised to see your family here," Crissanne said. "It's so nice that they came."

"They knew him, too. And they also know we'll need our support network around us."

"I don't have one," she admitted.

"You do now," he said, putting his arm around her.

As they stood there in front of the color photograph, she looked into Mason's eyes and she thought…he'd want her to be happy with Ethan.

Someone cleared his throat behind them and she turned to see the funeral director waiting there. "Are you ready to start letting everyone in?"

"Yes, sir," Ethan said. "I'd like to go over the

details with the minister who'll be conducting the service."

"He's back there," the director said, pointing toward a doorway to the left.

"Are you okay by yourself?" Ethan asked her. She nodded.

He left and the doors opened. Ethan's family were the first ones to come in. Crissanne noticed that Bianca and Kinley weren't in the crowd, which made sense with the kids. Hunter, whom she'd met a number of times, came over and introduced her to his wife, and Crissanne felt almost normal for a short while. She stood there in a crowd by herself but it was sort of comforting. Hunter had known Mason and reminisced about the times they'd had together, and it comforted her. It made it easier to let him go and helped her realize that she was moving on the way she should be.

As the service started, the sentiment she got out of all the stories everyone shared about Mason was that life was meant to be lived at full throttle.

She promised herself that starting now, she was going to live her life that way. No more hiding and pretending. Staring with Ethan Caruthers.

The walls of his bedroom in the house in Malibu were starting to feel like they were closing in on him. Ethan pushed the sheets off his body and got out of bed. The house was quiet now, but it had been full of people talking about Mason and celebrating his life earlier today.

It had been sobering in a way he hadn't anticipated. He'd spoken to many different people today, all about Mason. His friend had touched the lives of so many. It had humbled Ethan to think of what Mason had left behind. In his will, which Ethan had helped him put together, Mason had left his money to a charity that would fund inner-city kids' tuition to summer camps at the beach or in the mountains. Mason had always said that if he hadn't been sent to the mountains the summer he turned fourteen, he'd never have found his path.

Ethan scrubbed his hand over his chest, grabbed a pair of basketball shorts from the floor and pulled them on. Quietly, because his entire family was here and sleeping. He and Crissanne were sleeping in separate rooms. It had just felt like the right choice, but of course in the middle of the night, he regretted it. He missed her. He opened the door to the hall and made his way through the living room out onto the porch. The sky was bright and clear; the stars seemed to shine more brightly here in Malibu. He grabbed a bottle of Jack and headed down the stairs to the beach.

He hadn't been able to really say goodbye to Mason. Not yet.

Not until tonight.

He walked toward an outcropping of rocks and was surprised to see someone already sitting there.

Crissanne.

He hesitated. She'd probably come down here for the same reason. To say goodbye in private. The last thing he wanted to do was disturb her.

He'd been trying to keep his distance, had been doing that odd act of wanting her and needing her close, but also knowing that she needed space. Sex in the conference room had been what they'd both needed but it had felt…like a reaction to Mason's death more than something between the two of them. Sleeping with her in Cole's Hill was one thing but back here in Malibu, where she had been Mason's…

That had felt wrong.

He wanted whatever developed between them to be about them, not a reaction to their friend's passing.

He turned to go back to the house.

"Ethan, don't go."

He stopped and walked over to her where she was sitting on the outcropping. The tide was out so the beach was damp, but there wasn't any water lapping at the rocks.

"I didn't mean to disturb you."

"You're not. Just looking up at the night sky and talking to Mase."

Ethan sat down a respectable distance from her. He held up the bottle of Jack. "I came out here to toast him."

"I'll join you."

He lifted the bottle higher up in the air. "To good friends who will always live in our hearts."

Crissanne nodded. Ethan poured a measure of the whiskey on the ground for Mason before taking a swallow, and then he handed the bottle to her.

"Your turn," he said.

"To always living life on the edge," she said, then splashed a bit on the beach before taking a swallow and giving the bottle back to him.

He had another shot and leaned back on his elbow. They were both hiding from something. The truth was if Mason hadn't died and he'd come back to find that things had changed between Ethan and Crissanne, he might not have liked it.

"I'm not going to apologize to you for what's happening between us," Ethan said.

"Good. I don't want you to," she said.

"I feel guilty," he admitted.

She reached over and put her hand on his leg. "Don't. Mason and I were finished long before you and I kissed in Texas."

"But in my mind you weren't," Ethan said.

She tipped her head to the side, watching him in the moonlight. He wondered what she saw when she looked at him.

"Do you wish we hadn't hooked up?" she asked him.

"No," he said, his answer almost torn from him. "It's guilt, not regret. I want more with you and I wish that I'd been able to clear the air with Mason before we moved on together."

"Together? Are you sure?" she asked. "You've been…well, I wouldn't say running away because you are too smart for that, but there is a distance—"

"I know. I'm sorry. It's hard for me to be the man I want to be and the man I really am. You deserve my best."

"I don't have any complaints."

All of his life he'd had an argument or words for any situation. But with her, he felt like he was a first-year law student who couldn't do anything but quote back stuff he'd read in textbooks. "You should."

She shifted so that she was closer to him, then put her head on his shoulder. He wrapped his arm around her and something that had been tight and tense inside him finally relaxed.

He let out a long sigh and held her closer to him in the moonlight.

"The truth is I might have just moved out at the beginning of August, but Mason and I hadn't been a couple since January. I kept pretending I could just make it work if I stayed, but he kept leaving. I feel guilty, too," she admitted.

"Why?" he asked.

"Was I the reason he kept picking more dangerous places to film?" she admitted.

That hurt Ethan's heart. No one was responsible for Mason's decisions. "That boy was stubborn as the day is long, Crissy. He didn't do anything unless he wanted to."

She didn't say anything. She just put her hands over his wrist and they sat there until dawn sipping on the bottle of Jack and talking about their friend. They said goodbye in a way that had real meaning to the two of them and when dawn came, Ethan realized that he was ready to go back home.

Eight

Crissanne had fallen into a routine as the long summer days lingered in Cole's Hill. It was nearing the end of September and they'd been back from California for almost two weeks. Ethan's family had rallied around her, trying to cheer her up and make her part of the community. She'd even been recruited to the bachelor auction committee at the Five Families Country Club. Kinley had had to step down when her daughter, Penny, had gotten sick with pink eye and given it to her mom. They were both better now, but the end result was that Crissanne was helping with publicity.

And part of that was taking photos of all the bachelors in Cole's Hill. They were very diverse but she noticed one thing about Texas men: the confidence and humor they all brought to the table.

Today she was set up in the main lounge of the country club and was doing a brisk business with the members.

"This room always takes me back to my childhood," Bianca said as she walked in.

Having been a supermodel for years, Bianca was on hand to style the men, whose photographs would go into a booklet that would be sent to every household in Cole's Hill.

"Does it? Who are all these people?" she asked. "I mean, I read the plaques and I recognize the Caruthers name and the Velasquez name because of you, but the rest I'm not sure of."

"These are the members of the five families who founded Cole's Hill. The man in the middle is Jacob Cole. He gave the town its name. Next to him is Bejamina Little. She's Jacob's stepdaughter. She founded the first school in town. My ancestor Javier Velasquez was a rancher in this area before Jacob came. We had a land grant from the Spanish king. Next to him is Tully Caruthers and his sister Ethel. Jacob built her a house that stood where the clubhouse is now. Then there are the Abernathys. You'll meet Wil when he comes for his photo. He's funny and a bit of a flirt, so be warned. The last of the five families are the Grahams. Their ancestor is Bones Graham. He was the undertaker. His family turned the old homestead into a microbrewery on the outskirts of town. They are all reprobates."

"Talking about me, Bianca?" a man said from the doorway.

Bianca smiled over at him. "Of course not, Diego. Crissanne, this is my brother, Diego. He's harmless."

"Bi. No man wants to hear that. I'm a badass. Don't let my sister tell you any differently."

"A badass?"

"Yes," he said. "And many women find me appealing."

She had to laugh at the brother and sister bantering with each other. And surprisingly, the pang she usually felt when she was around families wasn't there. She had always thought she needed to be married or in a relationship to find a family, but she was slowly coming to realize that friendship was a strong bond.

"I'll reserve judgment until I see your photo," Crissanne said. "The camera always shows me the truth about someone."

"Uh-oh, Diego, you're in trouble now," Bianca said.

He mock-punched her and then moved farther into the room. Bianca's brother ran one of the largest stud programs in the United States. His horses were known for their speed and agility according to Nate, who had just signed a deal to have some of his mares covered by Diego's studs. She'd heard all about it at dinner a few nights ago.

"Give me a minute to adjust the lighting," she said. Originally, they'd toyed with the idea of having the photos taken at each bachelor's place of work, but it had been too hard to coordinate and Bianca had arranged for them all to come to the clubhouse instead. Crissanne had worked with the high school art department to design canvases to use as backdrops for the different men.

"One of your second cousins did this," Crissanne said. "Julia, I think."

"It's gorgeous," Diego said. "She's so talented. We're all very proud of her."

The five families had really put down roots here. Crissanne had learned as she'd been taking the photos that pretty much everyone—except for the newest residents of Cole's Hill—could trace their ancestry back to one of the five families.

Diego was easy to photograph. He smiled easily and wore his black Stetson well. He chatted with her the entire time, and when he left he winked at her as he walked out the door. She just shook her head and tried not to laugh.

As the day wore on, she was impressed by

the wide range of men who came to be photo-graphed. One of her favorites was Wil Abernathy. The rancher was more easygoing than Diego and didn't have the intensity of the other man.

Another bachelor who stood out was Manu Bennett. He had bulging muscles and posed with his shirt off, showing off his Maori tribal tattoos, which were distinctive to his family and covered his entire chest and back. He was tanned and muscled and it was only when he spoke about his brother and sister-in-law that she caught a hint of softness in his face. Otherwise he was intense and serious. She took her time making sure she cap-tured that essence of him.

"Only one more," Bianca said around five thirty. "Then a dinner break and the evening shift."

"I'm looking forward to going over the photos I took today."

"Me, too," Bianca said.

"Who's next?"

"I am," Ethan said from the doorway.

Ethan. She already had more pictures of him than she'd ever admit. But this was for the auc-tion, so she'd be careful to photograph him in a way that would make women want to bid for him.

She felt a pang of jealousy. She knew she didn't want Ethan going to anyone but her. But there continued to be a tentativeness between them, even as she'd begun to find her place in Cole's Hill. Which was why she was looking for her own apartment. They both needed some space to process Mason's death and then she hoped they'd be able to move on together.

"We can grab dinner when you're done," Ethan said.

Dinner.

"Like a date?"

He gave her a smile and she realized how much she'd missed him even though they'd been living together. "Yes, just like a date."

He'd been busy at work. Mason had wanted Ethan to be the director of his memorial foundation, and setting it up required a lot of time. In addition to that, he still had his regular law clients to take care of.

At home, he hadn't been sleeping because he'd reached out to Crissanne and then left the ball in her court. He wanted her in his bed, but he hadn't wanted to pressure her into sleeping with him.

He knew that since they'd come back from Malibu he'd been having a hard time dealing with the new thing with Crissanne and Mason's death. So he'd shut her out.

She was living in his house, trying to come to

terms with a new town, and he knew she needed time and space even though she said she was fine. He caught her in moments of sadness when she thought no one was watching.

"What do I need to do?"

Bianca had done her magic, styling his outfit so he looked as good as he could. But he loosened his tie after she left the room.

"Stand over there in front of the backdrop," Crissanne said, directing him to a corner of the room under the lights. She looked through her lens and then stepped back and set the camera down.

She posed him and took a series of photos. He followed her directions, but she soon stopped shooting and gave him a look.

"Relax."

"I am," he said. But really, had there ever been anything more uncomfortable than posing for a photo? He felt stupid. She'd told him to cross his arms and look confident, but instead he felt dumb.

"No, you're not. I've seen you more relaxed in the courtroom going up against a tough judge," she said.

"When?"

"In LA. Judge McConnell when you were doing that corporate case," she said.

"That was like four years ago," he said. He'd been trying to make a go at corporate trial law but it didn't suit him. The arguing did, but he preferred to settle out of court.

"Yeah, we had dinner afterward," she said. "Remember?"

"I do," he said, smiling as he remembered that night. "We ate at In-N-Out Burger because I didn't get out of work until late."

"We did," she said. "Mason was doing that heli-skiing thing in Canada and you said that we were friends, too, so we could hang out if we wanted to."

He noticed she'd started taking photos again. But he didn't really think of himself as her subject. He'd always liked to watch her work. She lost herself in the moment when she did. It was like she became someone else as she moved and talked.

She came over and moved his chin a bit, then kept taking photos. As he watched her, he realized that he'd been fooling himself for the last few weeks.

He'd been pretending he was giving her space when the truth was more complex. He'd been hiding from himself how much he liked her. Sex was one thing and actually more easily explainable to him. This emotion that he felt for her—well, that scared him. Because he'd never really know if she liked him for himself or if she'd just crashed into him when she'd been falling away from Mason.

"I think I've got something I can work with," she said. "I've never known you to look so tense, though."

"It's the entire bachelor auction thing," he said. "I know I'm not the only guy to feel silly that people are going to be bidding on me."

"I think it's a great idea. You should know that there is a lot of excitement in town about it," she said as she plugged her camera into her laptop and hit a few keys.

"Doesn't make me feel any less silly," he said. "Want to grab dinner now?"

She glanced over at him and smiled. She'd tied her hair back in a ponytail and the lipstick she'd had on earlier had worn off. "I would like that. I have to be back at seven thirty for another session."

"No problem. We can eat here at the club," he said. "In fact if you want to finish up I'll go and order a picnic dinner. I'll show you my favorite spot in this subdivision."

"Sounds good," she said, but her attention was on the photos downloading to her laptop. He approached and looked over her shoulder at his face on the computer screen. He hadn't realized how earnest he looked when he was talking. *What the hell?* He also hoped he was the only one who could see it, but the expression on his face made him look like he cared for Crissanne a lot. He knew that look. And it had been there for too long.

"What do you think?" she asked.

He didn't know what to say. And God, that wasn't like him. "You did the best with the subject matter."

She punched him lightly on the arm. "You're silly. I bet you're going to raise a lot of money. This photo is good. I'm not just saying that because I took it. I think it captures the essence of you."

"What is the essence of me?" he asked.

She tipped her head to the side and a strand of her hair fell forward against her cheek. "Honesty, integrity and a mouth that makes a woman think of long nights together."

Her words sent a shiver down his spine that made him feel every hour since he'd last held her in his arms. Since he'd kissed her and called her his own. It had been hard keeping his distance.

"You might see that," he said. "To everyone else I'm just that odd Caruthers."

"The odd Caruthers?" she asked.

"Well, the one who likes to argue," he added. What was he doing? He never talked about his place in his family. How he'd never really fit in.

She shrugged. "Maybe, but you're my favorite Caruthers."

The tension and the guilt that had been riding him since they returned to Texas fell back, and he knew that this was what he'd needed. Just being alone with Crissanne without the guilt that had been riding him hard. And he'd been afraid he'd pressured her into something but he was coming to realize that he hadn't.

Ethan was different as they walked along the golf course. He had been quiet since he saw the photos she'd taken of him. He had been her favorite to photograph today. Though she'd enjoyed the stories that all the men had told her with either their words or the expressions on their faces, Ethan was always going to be her favorite.

She'd been trying to find a place for herself here. A reason to stay that wasn't about liking Ethan. And she was pretty sure she finally had. She had projects to keep herself busy. She had mentioned to the committee chair of the Daughters of Cole's Hill that she thought they might be able to use some of the bachelors in a calendar. And the committee chair had agreed.

And she was ready to take the next step. Tomorrow she had an appointment to go and look at houses with a Realtor. If she was going to stay, she had to find her own place, not just move into Ethan's. It was something she'd thought about in

Malibu as she'd stood by the ocean many a night waiting for Mason to return from one trip or another before they broke up. Before he died. Now she realized that she'd spent her entire life waiting for someone to give her a home and she needed to find one for herself.

"You're quiet," Ethan said as he led her up the steps to a gazebo and they sat down on the bench.

"I was just thinking about Cole's Hill," she said.

"What about it?"

"I like it. I came here…well, I was running to you, not really thinking about the work I'd do. I mean, I knew I could sell a travel piece on the area, but I didn't have a plan. Vlogging wasn't working because I felt so lost," she said. She was rambling.

"You don't need a plan. You were in a bad place," he said.

"That's kind, but I always like to think of myself as an independent woman. When we were in Malibu I reflected a lot on my life with Mason. You know, I wasn't exactly dependent on him but I certainly was always waiting on a signal from him before I decided what I'd do next. I hate that," she said.

Ethan opened the picnic basket and handed her a plastic container and cutlery. "That's part of being in a relationship."

"Have you ever done that?" she asked.

He shrugged.

She'd never really considered it before but she'd never seen Ethan with a serious girlfriend. "Have you ever had a serious relationship?"

"Not really. I work too many hours and travel a lot. That's not really a good combination for a relationship," he said.

And yet that's exactly what she and Mason had had. "You're so right. I don't know why I couldn't see it before. Mason and I were both always leaving."

"It's hard to build something when you are both gone," Ethan said.

"It is. So is that all that's been keeping you back?" she asked.

"Where are you going with this?" he asked. He sounded defensive and a little bit guarded.

"I guess I want to know more about what makes you tick in the romance department," she said. "We've never talked about that."

"Why is that, do you think?"

"Maybe because I didn't want you to have a serious girlfriend," she said, quietly putting down her container and standing up and walking a few feet away from him.

He thought of all the years he'd spent watching

her and Mason from the sidelines and the envy that had been hard to manage at times.

"Is that why you've been keeping your distance since we got back here?" he asked.

She shook her head. "I was waiting for a signal from you. See my pattern? I don't know why I do that."

"I didn't want to pressure you," he admitted. "You are just settling in here in town, and then there's everything that happened with Mason. You need time."

"I need you," she said quietly, turning back to him.

Her words went through him, starting a fire that he didn't even try to ignore. He had done the right thing, the gentlemanly thing. He had spent every damned night of the last two weeks awake and aching, alone. Not really sleeping. Listening for any movement from her room and wanting her. Wanting to hold her, make love to her and claim her as his own.

He knew that she needed time. But time had always felt like an endless abyss to him. He knew that he didn't do well with waiting. Mason had always said it brought out the worst in him, and in honor of his friend's death, he'd tried to be better. But damned if he was.

He saw her standing there in the twilight as

the landscape lights came on, and he wanted her. The sun set behind her and the heavy, warm air stirred the fire.

He was tired of waiting. Tired of pretending that he was cool with letting her set the pace.

He stood up, holding his hand out to her, and she stepped forward and took it. "I'm tired of pretending with you," she whispered.

"Good," he said. He pulled her into his arms and kissed her like he'd wanted to since they'd left Los Angeles. She tasted better than he remembered and his arms, which had felt so empty for so long, held her close. He told himself to slow down, to gentle the embrace, but he couldn't. He wanted her and now that he held her he knew he wasn't ever going to let her go.

There were a million reasons to let her go, he thought. Her life was in transition and most likely, so was her heart. His ties were to Texas, but she might find life pulling her somewhere else.

But right now, nothing mattered except the way she felt in his arms and the way her mouth felt under his.

Nine

Crissanne let herself into Ethan's house using the key he'd given her. Bart and Ethan's housekeeper were both out of town for the weekend, and Ethan had needed to leave her at the country club when he got a call that one of his clients had gotten himself in trouble.

The house was quiet except for the subtle whir of the central air-conditioning. But then as she was walking toward the kitchen she heard a curse from Ethan's office and the sound of a glass shattering.

She hesitated, wondering if she should leave and let him have the house to himself tonight.

She hadn't even realized he was already home. But then she decided she was done with running. She'd run from Los Angeles to Cole's Hill, from Cole's Hill back to Los Angeles and from Mason to Ethan. And now she was here.

She was staying put. Wasn't that what today had been all about? Setting down roots in the community? She couldn't wait to talk with the Realtor—she'd already seen a listing for a small space in the historic district that she could lease for her office and photography studio.

She knocked on his door and saw him sitting on the large leather love seat between the bookcases with a glass of something that looked like whiskey in one hand and his laptop balanced on his knees.

There was a broken glass near the bookcase next to the wall.

He glanced up at her and smiled, but it didn't reach his eyes. Then he gestured for her to come in and she did, slipping her shoes off at the door. The floor was a beautiful Spanish tile, cool against her bare feet as she walked over to him. The room smelled of books and cigars and Ethan's cologne. As she got closer to him she noticed he had an earpiece in.

He hit a button on his keyboard. "Sorry, Crissy, I'm on a conference call."

"That's okay. You sounded pissed."

He shook his head and lifted his glass to his mouth and took a long swallow. "I work with idiots."

She had to laugh at the way he said it. Ethan was one of the smartest men she knew and normally so even-tempered. But not tonight.

"Can I do anything?" she asked.

He shrugged. "Not really."

She started to leave but got only halfway across the room before she glanced back and saw the way he was sitting there looking at the screen. Looking so alone. She realized that there were all kinds of running and this sort of isolation was Ethan's version.

She turned around, taking the cashmere throw off the back of one of the guest chairs and putting it on the floor at Ethan's feet. She sat down on it next to his legs, putting her hand in his.

He squeezed her fingers, and then put his hand on the side of her head, loosening her braid so that her hair fell around her shoulders. She tipped her head back to look up at him. He pushed a button on his laptop and set it aside.

He ran his finger down the side of her face, taking his time to carefully trace her cheekbones. Then she felt his finger move over her lips. She bit his fingertip and his eyes widened as he licked his lips.

She'd been waiting for him to make a move since they'd gotten back to Texas, but she'd soon realized that Ethan was too much of a gentleman to do that while she was sleeping under his roof and trying to figure out her next move.

But for now they were going to finish what they'd started in the gazebo earlier tonight.

She used his tie to pull him forward and kiss him. She loved the firmness of his mouth and how when it opened for her, the kiss would be soft. She teased him, keeping the kiss light when what she wanted was to straddle his lap and take him deep.

She wanted him but she didn't want to push intimacy on him when she knew he was dealing with guilt and pain at Mason's passing. Still, she ached for this. Being so close to Ethan and not having him was like seeing the…the very thing she wanted but knew she could never have.

She turned her head and rested it on his thigh as he sat back and pushed his hand deeper into her hair. He shifted his legs and she saw the ridge of his erection against his trousers. She stroked him through the fabric of his pants. He was hard and long, getting longer in her hand, and she realized how much she wanted him.

That ache that had been inside her every moment since they'd returned from California finally made sense. She'd wanted something that was almost within her reach. And it was within her reach right now. She drew her finger down the line of the zipper and then back up, watching him grow inside his pants.

He shifted, pushing his legs farther apart, and she moved between them, taking the tab of the zipper and drawing it down until she could reach inside his pants. He wore a pair of boxer briefs underneath his trousers and she found the opening in them, sliding her fingers through until she touched his hot flesh. She ran her finger up and down his length, taking extra time at the tip. She shifted again so that she was kneeling. She heard him start talking, but she knew it was his call. His voice was a low rumble as she undid the fastening at his waist and pulled his pants down slightly. He freed his erection from his underwear and she took him in her hand, leaning forward, her tongue darting out to touch the tip of his erection. His hand was at the back of her head, urging her forward until she took him in her mouth.

He thrust his hips and she felt him at the back of her throat as she moved her head up and down, her tongue teasing him as his hands moved over her neck and shoulders.

She pulled back and swirled her tongue around the top of his erection, stroking her hand down his length to cup him. He put his hand on her mouth, his thumb rubbing over her lower lip as he tilted her head back and their eyes met. Then he tossed his earpiece aside and lifted her up onto his lap.

She put her hands on his shoulders, pushing her fingers into his thick hair. This time when their lips met, he didn't let her tease him. His hand was on the back of her head, his fingers tangled in her hair, holding her head so that he could thrust his tongue deep into her mouth. She brought her teeth down lightly on his tongue before sucking on it as she rubbed her center against him. He groaned and she felt one of his hands moving down her back, pulling at the fabric of the dress she had on, tugging it up until he could get his hand underneath it. Then she felt his big, warm palm against the small of her back. He held her closer to him, his hips moving between her spread thighs, and she felt the tip of his erection against her center through the fabric of her skirt and her panties.

She pulled back, catching his lower lip between her teeth as she broke the kiss and shifted around in his arms, trying to remove her panties while staying on his lap.

He sort of laughed as she tumbled off his lap and he caught her, lifting her to her feet.

"Get naked, woman."

Yes. This was what she'd needed. This moment between the two of them.

She pulled her dress over her head and felt his hands on her naked breasts as she tossed the dress aside. She pushed her panties down her legs and then she was naked standing next to him. He was still wearing his shirt and tie, and his pants had fallen down to his ankles.

She looked up into his face. Their eyes met and the feelings she'd been trying so hard to bury overwhelmed her.

He was so dear to her.

She put her hands on his jaw and went up on tiptoe, kissing him hard, emotions roiling her like the jagged lightning that sometimes flashed across the big Texas sky. She felt his hands on her butt as he lifted her off her feet and carried her across his office. Then she felt the cold, hard surface of his mahogany desk under her.

Her nipples were rigid points and her breasts felt fuller. He kissed her hard and deep and then lifted his head and started to make his way down her body, biting at the point where her neck and shoulder met. Then he went lower to tongue one of her nipples while he lightly pinched the other one between his thumb and forefinger.

His mouth traveled farther down, until she felt the warmth of his breath against her most intimate flesh. He kept pinching her nipple with one hand while he parted her folds with the other. She felt his tongue flicking over her and she moaned, her head falling back as shivers went through her.

She held his head in her hands and let herself go, closing her eyes as he kept up the pressure.

"Do you like this?" he asked, his voice a low rumble, his lips moving against her body.

"Yes. Don't stop," she said. Her voice was husky and almost unrecognizable to her own ears.

"I'm not planning to until I'm buried deep inside you."

She shivered again as he continued to tease her clit with his tongue until she couldn't stop her orgasm. She tightened her thighs on either side of his head and held him to her as she arched her back and called his name.

She went limp in his arms as he kissed his way up her body to her stomach, his teeth biting gently into the flesh around her belly button. He continued trailing kisses up her body until he reached her mouth. Attempting to regain the advantage, she reached between the two of them, taking his shaft in her hands and drawing him forward until she felt the tip of him at her entrance.

He brushed his chest over hers, moving his hips to thrust deep inside her. She arched her back, tightening her thighs around his hips as he drove himself up and into her again and again. He held her with one hand in the middle of her back, and the other was braced on the desk beside her, his thrusts relentless, until she felt herself start to come again. She moaned as she felt him driving harder, deeper and faster, and then he came, filling her as he called her name. She wrapped her arms around him and held on to his shoulders as he continued to thrust three more times into her.

He pulled her off the desk and sank to the floor, cradling her on his lap. They were still intimately connected and she wrapped her arms around his shoulders, resting her head against his shoulder and neck.

He swept his hand up and down her back until their breathing quieted. Then he stood up and carried her out of the office up the stairs to his bedroom. Neither of them said a word as he put her on her feet next to his bed.

They took a shower together and then he climbed into his big bed with her and she turned on her side, looking up at him like she was searching for an answer to a question only he could provide.

"Thank you," he said, his voice sounding dry to his own ears. He said it simply to keep her from saying something real. Something that would remind him that sex with Crissanne—

"No, don't thank me," she said. "I'm not going to keep pretending there isn't this thing between us."

Thing.

Yeah, that was how he wanted their relationship to be referred to by the one woman he'd always wanted.

She shifted around, propping herself up on her elbow. "When I showed up on your doorstep it wasn't only because I had nowhere else to go. I wanted to be with you, Ethan. I was sad and lonely and I tried to think of the one place in the world that would make me feel better…"

She trailed off and his heart started to beat double time. He knew himself. Knew that if he let this woman into his emotions, into his heart, he was never going to be able to let her go. No matter what she said, he knew she wasn't in her right state of mind at this moment. She'd ended a more-than-a-decade-long relationship with her boyfriend, come to him, her boyfriend died, and now they were in bed together. Only a liar could convince himself this could be real.

And he wasn't about lying to himself. Not where she was concerned.

"Ethan?"

"Hmm…"

"What do you think about that? Are you glad I came to you?" she asked.

She needed something from him. Something he should definitely say to her. But what? The truth was he had dreamed of her in this bed with him for a long time. But he wasn't about to tell her that. He'd never thought of himself as a coward. He'd seen things and done things that most would say were brave, but when it came to being honest with Crissanne, something stopped him. Something made him hesitate because if he told her the truth and she rejected him...he'd have nowhere to turn.

Mason was gone.

His brothers had always seen him as the sanest one. The one who had his shit together. And now that they had all settled down and were working on families, he couldn't go to them all crazy.

He had to be smart.

"Ethan."

"Crissanne."

"Don't. Don't do this. I want to know what you're feeling."

"I don't know what I'm feeling," he admitted. "I know that sounds like a cop-out, but you have to remember that you and I have been friends a long time. I don't want to do anything to ruin that."

She shifted back, sitting up next to him and taking the covers with her. Pulling them up around her naked breasts. Which just made him remember how she'd looked naked in his office downstairs. *Hell.*

Now he was getting turned on again and she wanted to talk about feelings. He couldn't do it.

He wasn't going to do it.

He wanted her. He liked having her in his house. For now that had to be enough, because he wasn't sure what he'd do if she suddenly woke up and realized that she was ready to move on.

He tugged on the sheet.

She raised both eyebrows at him and scrambled to keep the sheet pressed to her body.

"I can't concentrate on anything but your breasts when you're naked."

She shook her head. "I know. That's why I'm covered up. I wanted to talk."

"We did talk," he said, wrapping his arm around her waist and tugging until she fell into his arms.

"Ethan."

He heard the longing and the insecurity in her voice, and he buried his head in her neck and took a deep breath. "I can't let you go."

"Really?"

"Yes," he said, pulling back and looking up at her. Their eyes met. "Can that be enough for now?"

She nodded, pulling him closer and hugging him to her. "It won't be enough forever."

"I know," he said, rolling onto his back and taking her with him. She was on top of him with the sheet wedged between them but their naked legs tangled together.

He put his hands on her face and looked up at her with that heartbreaking sadness and need and affection that she wanted to believe was love.

"Oh, Ethan," she said.

He didn't say anything, just kissed her fiercely, his tongue moving into her mouth. She pushed the sheets out from between them and straddled him, taking the only thing he'd freely give to her. She put her hands on his chest and shifted until he was at the entrance of her body, and then she slowly sank down onto him.

Their eyes met and her heart clenched as he wrapped his arms around her, thrusting up inside of her. She rode him not stopping until she felt him shuddering underneath her. She buried her head against his shoulder as her own orgasm washed over her.

It wasn't enough, she thought. She still wanted more. But this physical attraction between them was all he was willing to give her and for now she'd take it.

He held her as their breathing slowed, then

rolled to his side, tucking her close. She closed her eyes and drifted off and he held her in his arms, unable to sleep.

He wanted what was best for her. He wanted to see her smiling and happy. If that meant he kept her here in his arms, then that was what he'd do. If that meant he had to let her go when the time came, he'd do it. No matter how hard it would be.

But for tonight she was his. She was here in his arms and he wasn't going to waste a single minute of it.

He stroked his hand down her back and realized how empty he'd been before she came here. In the brief time that she'd been in his life this way, she'd become the one person he needed to see each day. The one person he needed to talk to each day. The one person he needed more than life itself.

Ten

The next morning when she woke up, Ethan was already gone. She sat up in the bed realizing that they still hadn't really found a way to talk about anything important. She loved being in his arms and sleeping with him, but if she'd learned anything in her relationship with Mason it was that there was more to being a couple than hooking up.

She glanced at the nightstand and saw a note. Of course. Ethan liked to leave handwritten notes instead of texting. It was kind of old-fashioned and yet at the same time suited to the man Ethan was.

She pulled the note off the table, rubbing the sleep from her eyes.

Crissanne—
Sorry I couldn't stay with you. I was tempted to call in but I need to get a deposition this morning. My folks want us to come to dinner at the Rockin' C tonight. My entire family will be there. Do you want to go? Call me later.
E

She leaned back against the headboard.

"What am I doing?" she asked the empty room.

But she knew she was going to say yes. Hot sex with Ethan was only part of the reason she liked him. She had to admit in all honesty she loved his family. They were in each other's business a lot of the time and he couldn't go anywhere in Cole's Hill without running into them. And the best part was they were treating her like she was one of their own.

Family had always been out of her reach and by coming here she'd gotten more than she'd bargained for.

But it was dangerous as well. If things didn't go well with Ethan she was going to have to leave. Cole's Hill was his town. The Caruthers were his family. And no matter how nice they were to her she had to remember that.

"Damn."

She got out of his bed and went down the hall to her bedroom to shower and get ready for the day. She was meeting the head of the bachelor auction planning committee to go over the digital proofs she'd shot yesterday, and she had an appointment to meet with the Realtor about that space downtown.

When she was all dressed, she sat down to look through the photos but found herself lingering over the ones of Ethan. He'd been tense when he'd first come into the session but then as he'd relaxed… She reached out to touch his face on her computer screen.

She had to be careful. She didn't want to screw this up the way she had every other relationship she'd ever had. Her heart felt heavy when she thought of hurting him, or even worse, never seeing him again.

She texted him that she'd love to have dinner with him and then mentioned she was looking at a space in town for her studio.

He texted her back that he was busy at work but would try to join her if she wanted a second opinion on the space.

Did she?

No, but seeing Ethan during the day would be nice.

She texted him the address and then put her phone in her purse and left the house.

When she got to the meeting she was surprised to see the room was full of about fifteen women. She hadn't been expecting a crowd, and was reminded that no matter how much goodwill had been given to her as Ethan's friend, she was essentially a stranger.

"Crissanne. Over here."

She looked over to see Bianca waving at her. She was seated next to Ma Caruthers and Kinley. Relieved to see some familiar faces, she made a beeline toward them.

"We saved you a seat," Kinley said.

"Thanks. I had no idea the committee was this large," Crissanne said, sitting down.

"I had the same reaction when I came the first time," Kinley said. "My boss Jacs donated my party-planning skills to the event, so even though I wanted to bolt for the door I didn't."

"I thought you grew up here," Crissanne said. Ethan had told her that Kinley's dad had been the foreman on the Rockin' C when Kinley was growing up and her mom had worked as a housekeeper for the Velasquez family.

"I did. Doesn't mean all these Five Families women don't intimidate me."

Crissanne had to laugh at the thought of Kinley feeling daunted around anyone. The younger woman was a dynamo, one of the most sought-after wedding planners in the country. And until last year, she had been a single mom.

"I can't believe that."

"Well, you should. Some of these women make me feel like I'm still wearing Bianca's hand-me-downs."

"They always looked better on you than on me," Bianca said.

"That's a big fat lie," Kinley said. "But thanks for trying to make me feel better about it."

"That's what friends do," Bianca said. "My mother might be coming later. She's up for a promotion at work so is spending more time at the station than usual."

"How's it going?" Kinley asked.

Crissanne sat there and realized that the nerves she'd first felt had disappeared. She had never experienced this before. While she'd never met Bianca's mother, the women were kindly including her in the conversation. And when Ma Caruthers turned toward them, she smiled warmly at Crissanne.

"Will we be seeing you for dinner tonight?" she asked around Kinley and Bianca.

"Yes, ma'am. Thank you for including me in the invite," she said.

"Not a problem. How are you adjusting to Cole's Hill? I know Bianca is going to tell us all once again how we live in the fastest-growing small town in the United States, but we're just a blip compared to Los Angeles."

"I love it. There's something so nice about the pace here," Crissanne said.

"Glad to hear it. And my son's not making you crazy yet?" Ma Caruthers asked.

"No, he's not," she said, but a part of her knew that he was making her a little...well, crazy. She wanted this to feel like home, like the place she belonged, and that connection was missing again. Was it her? Was it Ethan?

Ethan had spent the better part of the day working, trying to focus on his clients and not Crissanne. It was harder than he wanted it to be.

But as he headed for the Rockin' C that evening, he had nothing to distract him. Just the local country music station that seemed to be playing songs that made the ache in his gut even stronger.

When Blake Shelton sang about his wife naming the kids while he got to name the dogs, Ethan wanted everything to be clear-cut like that for him. But it wasn't. Yes, he wanted Crissanne. The sex between them was hotter than even he could have imagined, and he'd spent a lot of time over the years imagining it.

But there was something holding him back. He knew that in his mind he'd always believed that if they did get together it would just be perfect. So how did he explain the messy long pauses that he sometimes felt cropping up when they were talking? Or that awkward thing last night where he'd had to turn to sex to distract her?

When he looked at the relationships of other people in his life, they all seemed to go so smoothly. Even his dad, who was probably as close to a stereotypical laconic cowboy as a man could get, still managed to make his mom laugh. Some of Ethan's fondest childhood memories were of listening to the two of them talk on the porch after he'd gone to bed, their voices a low murmur through his open window.

He didn't have that easy rapport with Crissanne. Well, that wasn't precisely true. He felt it at times, but then he felt this crazy excitement at seeing her after a long period apart. This heady cocktail of needing to get her into bed and having her again and again so that maybe she would just get addicted to sleeping with him and that would be enough…for her.

He cursed and pulled off onto the side of the road.

Fear. That's what this was.

He'd always insulated himself from the things that would wound him. He'd used knowledge and arguments to keep anxiety at bay. But with her, there wasn't enough data he could accumulate to make him feel like she was a sure thing.

And why was it that he felt like this when his brothers all seemed to have nailed relationships with relative ease?

Someone honked and Ethan glanced in his rearview mirror as a pickup truck with the Rockin' C logo pulled to a stop behind him.

"Let it be Marcus," Ethan muttered to himself, hoping to see the former ranch foreman who had been recovering over the last year from a heart attack.

But no, it was Nate.

His big brother, who was always good for advice and a fight. He got out of his truck and walked toward Ethan's Ferrari.

He rolled down the window as Nate approached.

"That toy you call a car finally give up the ghost?" Nate asked. His brother had never been able to understand why Ethan had opted for speed and beauty over stability and strength.

"Nah. Just had to take a call and don't like to drive while I'm doing it," Ethan said. The lie was the first thing that had popped into his head.

"Yeah, right," Nate said. "What's really going on?"

"Nothing," Ethan said. "Why do you always do that? Question me?"

"Bro, I'm not trying to start anything. It's just there is absolutely no cell signal out here," Nate said.

Damn.

"Fair enough," Ethan said, putting his head forward on the steering wheel. Crissanne had even taken away some of his ability to be quick-witted when put on the spot.

"Ethan, you okay?" Nate asked.

"Yeah," Ethan said, then got out of the car to stand next to Nate because he wanted to feel less like a little brother at that moment. "I suck at relationships."

There, he'd said it. He knew admitting his faults was always a good place to start.

"Don't feel like the Lone Ranger there," Nate said. "I'm not that great, either. In fact, I'm out here because Kinley told me to take a hike for a while before she lost her temper."

Ethan smiled. "You two fight just to make up."

"Sometimes," Nate admitted. "But this was legit. Relationships are hard and they take a lot of work."

Was that true? "You make it look easy."

"That's because Mom raised us not to air our dirty laundry in public," Nate said. "That's why I'm out here riding the land while Kinley and Penny get ready for dinner. She needs a chance to cool down and so do I, or we'll have it out in front of everyone later on tonight."

"What's going on?"

"I want another kid," Nate said. "I didn't get to see Penny from birth and I think that we should jump right in and have another one before Penny gets too much older."

Kinley had raised Penny by herself until his niece was three because Kinley and Nate had lost touch; he hadn't even known he was a father. "Kinley wants to wait. Did she say why?"

"She wants to give the three of us a chance to really gel as a family, and I get it. I mean, I was a playboy and a douche. But I'm not going anywhere. I feel like she still sees the old Nate and is making me pay for what I said to her."

Ethan put his hand on his brother's shoulder. "She loves you. She might just want a chance for herself to feel secure. It's not always about you."

Nate threw his head back and laughed. "Derek said the same thing to me. Is my ego that big?"

"Sometimes," Ethan said, realizing that talking to his big brother had helped in a way he hadn't expected. "You told Derek?"

"Yeah, and Hunter…just between us, Ferrin is pregnant and he's going to announce it tonight," Nate said. "That's really what got me thinking about another kid."

"When the time is right it will sort itself out," Ethan said, not just to his brother but also to himself.

"I know. I just feel like I missed out on so much, I want it all and I want it now."

"I get that," Ethan said. "That's how it is with Crissanne." Ethan completely understood where his brother was coming from. Part of him felt that way with Crissanne.

Nate looked out at the horizon and then back at him. "I'm not trying to start anything but are you sure that you should be getting together with her this quick?"

"No."

"Well, hell," Nate said. "I mean, we all suspected you had a thing for her…but she was Mason's girl."

"Except Mason dumped her. Before he left on

the trip to Peru. So what does that say? All those years I stayed back so they could be happy…"

"Like I said, no judgment here. I just wanted to make sure you knew what you were doing. Ma said to leave it be. If you wanted to talk you'd come to us."

"Ma was right," Ethan said.

"Fair enough."

As he got back in the car and followed his brother to his parents' smallish two-story ranch house that they'd downsized to from the big house, he realized that he was closer to finding some peace about his feelings for Crissanne.

Ferrin Caruthers was a pretty professor at the University of Texas, the daughter of a famous college football coach. She'd married bad boy Hunter in a lavish wedding that Kinley had come to Cole's Hill to plan. It had been televised and viewed by millions on TV. So Crissanne wasn't sure what to expect when she met her, but Ferrin was down-to-earth and funny.

She was quieter than Kinley and Bianca but just as adamant that Crissanne should be part of their group. She hesitated to remind them that she and Ethan were…well, who knew what they really were. She liked him—a lot. And as soon as he'd walked onto the patio of his parents' house with his brother tonight, she'd felt that tingle go down her spine. She'd wanted to run over to him, but she'd made herself stay put.

She had to admit that the bond between the two of them was strong, but it seemed rooted in sex. Other than that, they had quiet night snippets of real conversations. She knew they were both not used to trusting others. Ethan, because of his career, where he saw people use the minutiae of the law to wiggle out of things. For her, it was thanks to the numerous group homes she'd lived in growing up.

But the truth was, she already trusted him.

She wouldn't have come to Cole's Hill when Mason dumped her if she didn't trust Ethan. And that's where her problems started. Were her feelings for him legit or was he just her safety net?

Could she live with herself if she treated Ethan like her safety net?

She knew that it would be difficult. She liked him and it was starting to feel like…love? She had no idea what love really was and she had no one to ask. She'd thought about bringing it up with Ethan's sisters-in-law, but they were all in solid relationships and seemed so much more together than she ever was. She should ask them for advice but she didn't know how to apply it. She wasn't the same as these women who knew their parents and came from the kind of families she could only dream of having.

Most of her life had been spent behind the camera capturing the important moments in others' lives, but never in her own.

She put the margarita she'd been drinking aside. She felt herself sliding into sad-drunk, which wasn't a good look on anyone and not what she needed to be tonight when she was dealing with Ethan's whole family.

Dinner was a barbecue. Ethan and his brothers stood around the pit with their father and the former ranch foreman, Quinten, who was Kinley's father. Benito and Penny were playing in the pool under the watchful supervision of Penny's British nanny, Pippa. She was a very pretty blonde who had jokingly said she needed to buy sunscreen in buckets.

They ate around a large table set under a pergola. Crissanne had been seated across from Ethan and as their eyes met she knew there were things she should say to him. But it was too much to mention at a family dinner.

For starters, she had to tell him she'd signed the lease on the shop in town and was going to move into the loft apartment above it. He hadn't been able to join her to look at the space after all.

She wanted to tell him before he found out from his mom, who had gone with her to check out the space. Ma Caruthers had treated her...well, in a way that had made Crissanne feel like she was part of the family.

She wanted that. But not at the expense of her friendship with Ethan. Her friendship, and whatever else was developing between them.

"I have an announcement," Hunter said, standing up and lifting his tequila glass.

"*You* have one?" Ferrin asked wryly.

"We have one," Hunter said, drawing his wife up next to him, wrapping his arm around her. As the two of them stared into each other's eyes, Crissanne realized that was what she wanted. She wanted Ethan to look at her the way Hunter was watching Ferrin.

Like she was the beginning and the end of his world. Like she was all that mattered. And Crissanne, who'd always been passed on by prospective adoptive parents and whose more-than-a-decade-long relationship had ended in, well, a crash and burn, really wasn't sure she was worthy of that look. That anyone would have that kind of desire for her.

Especially someone like Ethan. She had always suspected that he was attracted to her but now she knew it was more than attraction.

"Ferrin and I are going to be parents," Hunter said.

There was a whoop of joy and everyone raised their glasses to drink a toast. Crissanne joined everyone else in giving Ferrin and Hunter a hug, but Crissanne felt the reality of her place here when someone asked her to take a photo of the family.

Once again, she was on the outside looking in.

She shook the feeling off and went inside to grab her camera instead of using the smartphone. When she came back, she took several photos.

Looking at the world through her camera balanced out her emotions. Gave her the perspective she needed.

"It's time," Pa Caruthers said when she was done taking pictures.

There was some groaning as the men watched their dad trying to work his smartphone. "Someone come and show me how to make this thing play music."

As Nate helped his father, the women all shook their heads. But then applause came out of the speakers, followed by the low country drawl of Waylon Jennings. It was "Good Hearted Woman."

"Brace yourself," Ferrin said. "This is the Caruthers family song."

Winston Caruthers started singing along with Waylon, and then Hunter came in on Willie Nelson's part. Before too long all five Caruthers men were singing along. Then they all started to come over and claim their women. Ethan reached for Crissanne and for a brief moment, she really felt like she finally had someone she could call her own.

Eleven

Ethan hadn't meant to drink as much as he had or to dance with Crissanne until after midnight, but then, nothing went the way he planned with her. And they were still at it. Now Niall Horan's "This Town" was playing, and unlike earlier on the drive over when Ethan hadn't been able to relate to the song on the radio, this one made him realize exactly what he wanted from Crissanne.

"Why are you watching me like that?" she asked.

"Just figured out the answer to a question that has been bothering me for days," he said.

"What is it?"

"I think…I really care for you," he admitted, dancing her off the patio and toward the garden that was his mom's pride and joy.

The path was illuminated with lights placed every five feet along its length. The smell of jasmine and roses combined in the air and Ethan took a deep breath, looking up at the night sky so clear and wide and full of stars tonight. It seemed like the truth was finally in front of him.

Everything came back to Crissanne.

He'd been afraid to admit it until now.

"I care for you, too," she said softly as he led the way to the bench near the fountain at the center of the garden.

He heard the party still going on behind them but it faded as they moved farther into the garden.

"I'm sorry I missed going with you to see the studio space in town today," Ethan said. He wanted a clean slate to start before he said what was in his heart. It had been there for a while now but he'd been afraid to admit it. But then he dived right in.

"I always think that I have this ordinary life where I'm not very tempted by anything and there is no fear. But with you, Crissy, I question that."

"What do you mean?" she asked.

"I am so unsure of myself with you. I mean,

I know I want you and having you live with me over the last six weeks has been, well, better than I expected," he said.

"It's nice for me, too," she said. "But there is something I wanted to talk to you about. I mean, it's hard to really give our relationship the right perspective when we are always together."

What was she getting at?

Had he found his way to her but only too late?

They sat down on the bench. He was silent for a moment as he looked around at the plants and flowers, whose petals were mostly closed for the night. "My parents moved out here a little more than three years ago and my mom started working on this garden."

"That's nice."

"Yeah, she had never had one because she was busy being a ranch wife. Cooking for the hands with our housekeeper, running kids to school and serving on committees in town. But when dad retired and they moved here she said that she realized her entire life had been building toward this."

"It's very pretty. Why are you telling me this?"

"I've never felt that my life was building toward anything," he admitted. "I'm a senior partner in the firm but that's not what Mom was referring to. She's talking about the bigger picture. I've never had that feeling of achieving my dreams in my personal life…until you."

She stared at him without answering. Was that fear in her eyes? Hope?

"I know it's too soon for this. We haven't had a proper courtship or done any of the things that couples should do. But for me when I think about my life and the future I realize I'm picturing you by my side."

"Ethan—"

"Don't say anything. I'm just telling you where I am. I know you're not in the same spot," he said. How could she be? She'd broken up with Mason and then he'd died. And she'd moved her entire life from California to Texas.

"The thing is, I might be," she said. Her voice was soft, and she looked over at him before taking his hands. "I need to tell you something before you find out from someone else."

"What?" he asked, not sure what she had just said. Did she want a relationship with him? Was she happy to just keep things as they had been?

"I signed the lease on the studio in town and the loft apartment above it today. I am going to move into the apartment this weekend," she said.

She was moving out of his house.

"Why? There's plenty of room at my place," he said.

"There is and there isn't," she said. "Everywhere I look it's your house. I feel like I belong there, but I don't know if I do. Does that make any sense?"

"No," he said. "I like having you in my house."

"I like it, too, but I like you more, Ethan. I think I could really care about you and I don't want to let myself get sucked into not believing in us because you are offering me something I've always wanted. I've never had someone to call my own, really my own. Living with you here would be solid and real and that scares me."

"What?" he asked. "What is it that I represent that you are afraid of?"

"Home."

Just one word and he couldn't argue with her anymore. He got it. She needed space to be sure. The same way he needed her in his bed every night and to wake up next to her each morning to feel secure. She needed that apartment of her own.

"Do you want me to give you space?"

"No," she said. "I was hoping we could date and try this like real people."

Real people. He wasn't sure that there was one way that was more real than another, but if she needed to live in town to feel like she had her own space, then he couldn't argue with her. She'd been sharing a home with Mason for a long time and that hadn't brought her the relationship she wanted. He could be the bigger man and give her space.

But he hated it.

He felt that if he let her go now she'd just slip away from him.

"Okay. I'll help you move this weekend," he said.

"I was hoping you'd say that," she said.

Ethan had been as good as his word, even going as far as asking his decorator to use his accounts at the different furniture stores in the area to make sure that she had everything she needed.

Right after moving in, Crissanne had to take a trip to New York to meet with a brand that wanted to work with her, and she'd left with the belief that her apartment would be boxes and a mess until she had a chance to sort it out. But Ethan had taken care of everything.

When her flight arrived today, he'd come to pick her up at the airport and drive her to the apartment. Now, as she opened the door, she was surprised to see that the decorator had gotten everything in place as they'd discussed.

"What do you think?" Ethan asked, carrying in a box of photos that she'd been storing in his garage since she'd moved out of Mason's house.

"I love it. I can't believe how finished it is," she said. She walked farther into the room. It smelled of the ocean and sunny summer days, no doubt thanks to the plug-in air fresheners, she thought as she slowly went from area to area. The only permanent wall in the loft was one that divided the bathroom from the rest of the space. There was a screen that she'd ordered that created a separate bedroom from the living area. And Bart had come out to build a low counter on one edge of the kitchen area. The floors were all hardwood and the window treatments were sumptuous yet modern.

The entire place fit her aesthetic in a way she hadn't realized it would. She'd always had an eye for what went together from framing scenes to be photographed, but this was the first home she'd ever had all to herself. The first place that she could call her own.

She was slightly overwhelmed at it as she looked around.

"Thank you," she said to Ethan.

"All I did was supervise and make sure that everyone followed your instructions," he said. "I like it."

"Thanks. I wasn't sure if it would all come together or be a mess. In my head I saw it one way but this is so much better."

He laughed. "Ellen was very impressed with your skills and suggested if you wanted to stop being a photographer she'd hire you at her interior design company."

Crissanne shook her head. "I don't think I'd like it. This was so personal."

"Where do you want this box?"

"Just put it over there in the living area," she said. "I have to figure out which pictures I want to put on the walls."

"I'll go and get the kitchen stuff while you do that," Ethan said. "Bart said he'll be stopping by later to finish up the island in the kitchen."

"Yes, he is a really good worker," Crissanne said. "I was a little hesitant at first when I heard his story but I should have factored in the Ethan effect."

He shook his head. "I'm not sure I want to know what that is."

"Just how you bring out the best in everyone. I think it has to do with the way that you see people without judging them."

He blushed, which she thought was cute. There was something about having Ethan here in her place that made her realize how much she was going to miss living with him. But they both needed this. She wanted to be sure that what she felt for him wasn't just about having a nice house and good people around her. She wanted to make sure her feelings were for *him*.

She already suspected they were, but this would help.

"Who am I to judge?" Ethan asked. "I'm just a litigator."

"You are a good man," she said.

He shrugged and left the loft, and Crissanne turned back to her box of photos. She sat down on the floor next to it and opened the lid. The first framed photo she pulled out of the box was one of Mason and Ethan that she'd taken while they were all still in college. The two of them were arguing about something while sitting in the quad. They'd been so intent on making their points—both of them—that she'd actually been able to get an entire series of shots before they noticed her.

She leaned the photo against the large square wood coffee table and pulled another photo from the box. Most of them were of Ethan, Mason or shots she'd taken on the job. She'd been nominated for a few awards over the years and would put those photos in her office downstairs along with the awards.

But she'd have to figure out where to place the private ones in the room.

"I remember that day," Ethan said quietly as he came over to where she was.

She glanced at the picture propped against the coffee table. "What were you two fighting about?"

He lifted the framed fifteen-by-seventeen-inch photo off the floor and held it in both of his hands as he looked at it.

"You."

"What? Why?"

"I thought that Mason wasn't giving you what you needed, that he was pushing you toward a career in travel photography because it suited him and his lifestyle more than you," Ethan said.

She just stared up at him. He'd been right, of course, but then again when wasn't Ethan correct? It had been one of the things that she and Mason had fought about over the years. He liked that she worked away from home. Liked that she traveled at least as much as him.

He had said it was so neither one of them was home all alone, but now looking back she realized it was so that they didn't get too used to having the other around.

"I do like my job," she said.

"Do you? I think you like the idea of having the studio here in town," he said. "I'm glad you've settled here in Cole's Hill."

She looked up at him and knew that the reason she'd come to Texas had been more complicated than she'd wanted to admit. But her reason for staying seemed to be centering on Ethan.

Later that afternoon, Ethan's parents, along with Derek, Bianca, Hunter and Ferrin, had all stopped by to bring housewarming gifts and help out with different tasks. Ethan had been dealing with all sorts of emotions since Crissanne told him she wanted to move out, but seeing her in her own place and so happy had just confirmed that it was the right move for her.

And for him.

He'd never talked about Mason in anything but glowing terms. If she'd stayed with him, there would have been no point. Even now, Ethan didn't really want to speak ill of the dead, but there had always been a part of Mason that was focused on what he wanted and what he needed from those around him.

He had one time told Ethan that he pictured his entire day and who he'd run into and what he needed from that person. It was one of the things the two men had in common. They both were able to look at the world and see their own path so clearly.

But while Ethan saw his path now with Crissanne, it was becoming more and more clear to him that Mason had seen a solo path for himself.

He just hadn't known how to break free of Crissanne.

When she'd first shown up on Ethan's doorstep, he thought it was temporary. A lover's quarrel that would be resolved in time. But he realized now that would never have happened. Maybe he was making assumptions about Mason's mindset when he broke up with Crissanne that could never be confirmed now that Mason was gone. But when he really thought about it, Ethan was pretty damned sure that his best friend wouldn't have minded his relationship with Crissanne.

"Got a minute, Eth?" Hunter asked him while they were all in the kitchen making sandwiches for lunch.

"Yeah, what's up?"

"Nothing big. Just wanted to talk to you alone."

"You can use my office downstairs," Crissanne said with a smile.

"Thanks," Ethan said, leading his brother down to the office.

"Sorry to do this today but Ferrin and I have to head back to College Station this afternoon and I thought it would be better to talk in person. I don't know what I have to do to legally protect Ferrin in case something happens to me. Since we got married last year I named her as my beneficiary, but I think I need to do more."

Ethan handled the estate planning for his whole family, not just for their individual accounts but also for the family trust and ranching business. "You're all set up as far as the family trust and the accounts for the Rockin' C Corporation are concerned. She'd get your shares upon your death and I've set up a separate trust for your child when he or she turns eighteen. Do you want to do something different?"

"I don't know," Hunter said. "I hadn't even considered it until Ferrin mentioned how young Mason was when he died and I thought hell, we don't know that we'll be given tomorrow, you know?"

"I do know," Ethan said.

He spent the next hour going over estate planning details with Hunter and reassuring his brother that everything would be taken care of.

"I spent so much of the last few years just focused on the past and clearing my name that this is sort of weird. I never thought I'd have Ferrin or a baby or anything like this," Hunter said.

"I know. But you deserve this happiness and I'll do everything I can legally to keep your worries at bay," he said.

"I know you will, Eth," Hunter said. "What's the deal with you and Crissanne? I like her. I think she's good for you."

"Good for me?"

"She got you dancing the other night instead of just sitting around and drinking or starting a fight with someone," Hunter said.

"I like her, but she's… I think she's at a crossroads," Ethan said, trying to explain something that he wasn't sure he understood. He was doing his best to give her what she needed. To not take anything for himself, which he was only just realizing was his usual mode with her. He always saw her as out of his reach and it wasn't lost on him that the one time she was actually in his arms he'd let her slip away again.

"What crossroads?" Hunter asked.

He took a deep breath and finally admitted what had been swirling around his mind for too long. That his best friend was always going to be between them. No matter that she'd left Mason before the other man had died, a part of Ethan would always feel guilty that he was sleeping with his best friend's girl.

"Somewhere between me and Mason," Ethan admitted.

"That's BS. She was always on her own with Mason. His hold on her was tenuous."

Ethan didn't believe that for a moment. Why would she have stayed with Mason so long if she hadn't wanted it to work out with him?

"Maybe. Whatever. She's here now and we are going to try to date and stuff like that."

"Ha."

"Ha?"

"Yeah, you always try to manage everything, but love isn't like that."

"I didn't say I loved her."

"You don't have to," Hunter said. "When she laughs you smile."

Ethan hadn't realized that. "I…"

"Don't deny it. No one knows more than I do how much falling for a woman can mess with who you think you are. But Ethan, from the other side, let me tell you that it is worth it. Ferrin has brought something to my life that I never dreamed I'd have. And I think Crissanne can do that for you, if you let her."

He didn't know how to respond to that and luckily Hunter let him change the subject. But after his family went home and it was just him and Crissanne, he had to admit that he was falling in love with her.

Twelve

Ethan helped her clean up after the party and then went home. And just like that, she was alone. Suddenly she understood why she'd stayed with Mason for all those years despite the fact that the relationship had been over for a while. She really didn't like being alone, despite the fact that she spent so much time by herself. It didn't matter that the apartment had been decorated by her and was her home now. It felt the same way as whatever small little room she'd been assigned when she'd been growing up and moving from house-to-house.

Too big and too empty.

She had all this space but was once again alone with no one to help her fill it. She wanted someone in her life. Someone she could trust and build a family with. She wanted that man to be Ethan.

She reached for her phone and started to text him. But how could she determine her true feelings for him if she kept leaning on him like a crutch? She got up and went to her laptop on the kitchen table and got back to reviewing the photos she'd taken over the last week.

The faces of Cole's Hill were starting to become so familiar to her. There were little details of people's lives that she had gotten to know through working with the women's group to photograph the bachelors and talking to the people she'd stopped to photograph in the park. Unlike Los Angeles, where everyone was essentially a stranger, these people were her neighbors.

She wanted this to be her home. She'd fought for so long for this that she knew she was going to make it work.

There was a knock on her door and she got up from the table, leaving a photo of Ethan enlarged on the screen.

She looked through the security peephole and caught her breath.

It was him.

"Hello, you," she said, opening the door.

"Hiya," he said, holding up a bottle of chilled Moët. "I know it's your first night alone and everything, but I thought we could have a toast and maybe talk."

"I almost texted you," she admitted, standing back so he could come in. "But then I felt silly because I was the one who moved out. Shouldn't I be able to stand on my own?"

"Who says you're not?" he asked. "I brought you a little something."

She opened the door further and he stepped inside. When he walked over to the kitchen table to put down the bottle of champagne, he looked at his photo on the computer.

"It's for the auction."

He just nodded and grabbed a towel from the kitchen counter to open the champagne. "Aren't you curious about your present?"

"I am."

She went into the kitchen after him, taking a seat at the breakfast bar and drawing the Neiman Marcus box he'd set down toward her. "You have already done so much for me, you didn't need to get me another gift."

"I wanted to," he countered.

He popped open the bottle of champagne and

then came over to stand on the other side of the counter from her. "Open it."

She carefully opened the box. Inside there was a pair of champagne glasses with gold leaf on them that spelled out her name.

She stared at them knowing she needed to thank Ethan but unsure if she could. He'd given her something she wouldn't have thought to ask for. It might seem silly to think that as a thirty-year-old woman she'd never really had things that felt like they were part of building a future, but she hadn't. She'd lived in the now with Mason because that was what he liked. And in her childhood, she'd taken nothing with her from the homes where she'd lived. All she had from that time was the Brownie box camera she'd bought at a second-hand shop before leaving for college.

"Ethan…"

"They were supposed to be delivered this morning but of course didn't arrive until tonight. I wanted you to toast your new home with your glasses."

"I'd love that."

Ethan rinsed the glasses and dried them while she sat there on the stool making small talk about the upcoming bachelor auction.

"I was surprised to hear this is your first year participating," she said.

"I almost always plan a trip around this time of the year so I'm not here when it happens. I make a donation and don't have to go up on the stage."

"But not this year?" she asked.

He shook his head. "I had that trip planned but it…got canceled."

With Mason.

"Do you feel like there is ever going to be a moment when Mason isn't between us?" she asked after a long silence.

He tipped his head to the side and arched one eyebrow at her as he poured the champagne.

"No. He's been a part of our lives for too long."

He had been. But she was starting to resent his presence in a way because he was keeping both her and Ethan from letting down their guard. She was tired from traveling today so couldn't analyze it properly, but she knew there had to be a way for them to step out from the long shadow cast by their friend.

"To your first home and the start of your adventure in Cole's Hill," Ethan said, raising his glass toward her.

She clinked her glass against his and took a sip, closing her eyes for a moment.

"To good friends."

"I want to be more than friends," he admitted to her.

She did, too. "I want to be sure, Ethan. I don't want to hurt you. It's only fair to you."

He glanced around the apartment.

"This place?"

"Your town, your family, it's everything I've secretly wanted for so long."

Ethan put his glass down and walked around the counter, not stopping until he turned her on the stool to face him.

"You're all I've secretly wanted. And if it takes you living on your own to convince you that we are meant to be together, then so be it."

They decided to watch a movie with superheroes in it that didn't hold his attention. Every time she reached into the bowl on his lap for some popcorn, his body responded. He wanted her, but she'd moved out and any man with half a brain would realize she needed space to think.

"I guess I should be going," he said when the movie finally ended.

"Not yet," she responded, turning to face him on the couch.

"If I stay we are going to be doing our version of Netflix and chill," he said, lifting his head to meet her stormy gray gaze. "Are you sure you want that?"

"I'm not sure about anything," she admitted

quietly, tangling her hands in his hair. "But I want you, Ethan, and being apart hasn't changed that."

A pulse of desire went through him, shaking him to his core. She shifted on the couch, straddling his lap to kiss him. He realized how much he liked her hands on him. Rubbing her back, he slipped one hand under her shirt, loving the feel of her bare skin. She was so natural about everything she did.

That was a turn-on in itself. But then, everything about Crissanne was. He'd wanted her from the first moment they'd met. But he'd been cautious and for once he wondered if that wasn't the way he should be. She was bold, taking chances and reaching for him even though she wasn't sure. He wanted to have every detail locked down and secured before he gave her any more of his heart. But maybe that wasn't the way to go.

All he knew was that right now, he was glad to have her in his arms.

"I think I want you to spend the night here," she said. "Will you do that?"

"Sure."

"And since tomorrow is Sunday that means I don't have to wake up to a note," she added.

She meant for him to stay in bed with her, wake up with her lazy-Sunday style, and he wasn't sure he could do it.

"Uh, of course," he said.

"What?" she asked, and as she straddled his lap and looked straight into his eyes there was no place for him to hide.

"If I stay it's going to be even harder for me to give you space," he answered. "Already I hate that you moved into town without me."

She chewed her lower lip and sat back on his thighs, shifting away from him. "Me, too. But I needed to do it. I had to prove to myself that I am strong without you."

"Did you do that?" he asked.

She shook her head. "Not yet. All I proved is that I am stubborn and won't give in to things that tempt me. You tempt me, Ethan Caruthers, but I don't want to push you away."

"Me, either."

She stood up and held her hand out to him and he followed her across the loft to her bed. It was queen-size with a plain cream-colored bedspread. She stopped there next to it and he pulled her close, singing under his breath the words to Eric Clapton's "Layla," because if ever there was a woman who'd been his obsession for his entire adult life it was Crissanne.

Even having had her in his bed, he still felt like she was just out of his reach. His Layla. And he didn't want that anymore. Sure it would be smart and sensible to give her space and let her make her own way back to him, but as Hunter and Nate had both warned, love didn't follow the sensible path.

She wrapped her arms around his back and rested her head on his chest as he sang and danced her around the room. And he knew that he loved her. He might have been trying to play it like he just really liked her, but the truth was, he loved this woman.

She stumbled on the bedside rug and they tumbled back onto the bed, both of them laughing.

"Dang it, woman, all you had to do was ask and I'd have gotten in your bed."

"My way worked," she said, still giggling. "Now get naked."

"Get naked?"

"Yeah, it feels like forever since I've seen you naked," she said.

"Only if you get naked, too," he said.

"Deal."

She hopped off the bed, shimmying out of her skirt and pulling her tunic over her head, and all he could do was lie there and watch. She was tanned and her waist was nipped in, her hips full and her legs so long. She glanced over at him.

"Uh, nothing else is coming off until I see some skin, Caruthers."

He pulled his T-shirt over his head and tossed it aside. "How's this?"

"Not bad," she said, reaching over to caress his chest. "But keep going."

He sat up and snaked his arm around her waist, drawing her forward between his legs and then falling back on the bed so she was on top of him. He found her mouth with his and kissed her long and hard and deep. Using one hand, he undid the back of her bra. Feeling it come free, he slid the straps down her arms until it was caught between their bodies.

He felt the tight beads of her nipples against his chest and groaned as she tore her mouth from his and used her hands on either side of his head on the bed to push herself up, grinding her crotch against his. She started to shift away but he put both hands in the back of her panties, cupping her butt and holding her to him.

"That's cheating," she said.

"Objection," he said. "Now we are both topless."

"Counselor, that is pushing it," she said. "I want you out of those jeans."

"I'm holding something I don't want to let go of," he argued.

"I'll make it easier for you," she said, rolling to her side. He let her go, slowly drawing his hands up her back and caressing her breasts as she shifted away from him.

He got to his feet and pushed his jeans and underwear down his legs, completely forgetting about his shoes, which he toed off last. Then he turned back to her, completely naked.

"I think you need to take those panties off," he said.

He glanced up to see her watching him. She pushed her panties down her legs and then stepped out of them. She took him in her hand, stroking him, until he was pretty sure he couldn't get any harder.

He tumbled her onto the bed again, careful to make sure that his weight didn't come down on her. Then he shifted around on the bed until he leaned back against the headboard, putting his hands on her waist, lifting her onto his lap.

She shifted backward on his thighs, stroking her hand up and down the length of his erection. If he got any harder he thought he might explode, and he didn't want to do that until he was buried inside her sleek body.

He brought her hand to his mouth and pressed a hot kiss in the center of it before nibbling his way up her arm to her shoulder. Then, cupping her breasts, he lowered his head.

Her breasts were full and pretty with their pink

nipples that stood out against her tanned skin. He plumped them up and rubbed his thumbs over them until they peaked and hardened under his touch. Then he leaned forward and sucked one of them. She put her hands on his shoulders, her nails digging into his skin.

Her fingers caressed the back of his neck in a light teasing pattern that sent shivers down his spine and made his hips jerk forward. But he was determined to make this night last. This was the first time he was making love to her when he knew he loved her. Admitting it to himself had been a long time coming, and he wanted this to last.

But Crissanne was the only argument he had when he thought about defending his life. Slow might be what his mind wanted, but his body had different ideas. She shredded his self-control and left him desperate for more. More of her mouth. More of her body. More of her touch.

She moved over him, her warm center rubbing the tip of his erection as she shifted position.

He lifted his head from her breast and looked up at her. She stared at him for a long time and then leaned forward to kiss him as he slowly entered her body.

He gave over control, letting her slide down on him until he was fully inside her. He reached between their bodies and flicked his finger over her clit, feeling her surprise as she tightened on him. Then as he continued to caress her, she started to rock against him.

He put his hands on her waist and slowed the movement, trying to draw it out, but she buried her fingers in his hair again, forcing his head back as her mouth took his. Damn, he loved the way that felt. She bit his lower lip and sucked it, then followed that with her tongue in his mouth. The kiss was carnal and raw, and he stopped thinking of anything but the way she felt in his arms.

He thrust his hips forward, driving himself deeper inside her. And still it wasn't enough. Tearing his mouth from hers, he noticed that she'd braced her arms on the headboard and her breasts were right in front of his face in that position. He turned his head and sucked her nipple, while simultaneously putting his hands on her hips and urging her to ride him harder and faster.

Still he couldn't get deep enough, couldn't take her fast enough or hard enough, the way his gut was churning for him to do. She threw her head back, gripping his shoulders as she moved on him with more urgency. He felt a jolt in his body and suddenly he came. He'd wanted to wait but as he thrust up into her one last time, he felt empty. He couldn't help it.

Then she tightened on him. Her inner core gripped him, her nails biting into his shoulders and his name a loud cry on her lips as she shuddered in his arms and then fell forward to his shoulder. Her breath brushed over his neck and chest.

He stroked his hands down her back, tracing the length of her spine. She turned her head, looking up at him with those big storm-gray eyes of hers, and he felt a punch near his heart. Tonight, everything was different. Making love to her in this strange apartment confirmed what he'd been afraid to admit until tonight.

He rolled to his side, holding her close to him.

"So we're sleeping in tomorrow?" he asked. Trying to talk when he felt like he wanted to confess his feelings was hard.

"Yes," she said.

"I'll try," he said. Staying here with her was at once the only thing he wanted and the very thing he was afraid of. What if he told her he loved her and she wasn't ready? What if…

She curled up on her side and put her hand over his heart, dropping a kiss on his chest and sleepily saying good-night.

His fears receded as he held her.

Thirteen

Crissanne's phone rang at 2:00 a.m., which made them both groan. She reached for it and knocked the alarm clock off the nightstand instead. Nothing was where she remembered it being.

"It's your phone," Ethan said, getting out of bed and padding naked across the loft to where she'd left her phone charging on the kitchen counter. He turned off the TV as he brought the phone back to her. It had stopped ringing and he handed it to her without a word.

As she hit the unlock button, Ethan's phone pinged with a text message, too.

But that barely registered. Because when she looked at hers, she saw that the missed call was from Mason.

His picture was on her screen, and she couldn't help the tears that burned her eyes as she lifted the phone to her ear and listened to the voice mail. Someone had probably found his phone and was trying to get back in touch with whomever had lost it.

"Shit," Ethan said, reading his text.

The voice mail started at the same moment he cursed. There was static, followed by a man's voice. "Cris, it's me. I'm alive. We need to talk. Call me."

She dropped the phone on the bed. Mason? Mason alive? She shook as she wrapped her arms around her body and then glanced over at Ethan.

"Mason is alive," Ethan said.

"I know. He left me a voice mail," she said.

Oh. My. God.

"I can't be here," Ethan said.

"Why not?" she asked. She didn't like the panic she saw on Ethan's face. And the guilt.

"It's not right. He's been injured. His text said he's still got a cast on his left leg and his ribs aren't healed yet," Ethan said. "You need time to figure out things with him. Without me in the middle."

Crissanne stared at the man who'd come to

mean more to her in six weeks than Mason had meant to her in twelve years. And he was telling her he needed to give her space.

"No. Ethan, I don't think running from my place in the middle of the night will help anything."

"He's on his way to see me," Ethan said.

"What?"

"That's what his text said."

"Okay. Let's both go and see him. I can't believe he's alive."

"Me, either."

"I'm glad," she said. "He was too young to die."

"He was—is," Ethan said, moving around and gathering his clothes.

And in that moment, all the joy and affection that had been between them before was gone.

There was a flatness in her apartment that hadn't been there before. She felt uncomfortable being naked, so she got out of bed and went to her dresser to pull on jeans and a sweatshirt. When she turned back around, Ethan was standing in the living area of her loft on his phone texting.

This didn't feel right.

"We need to talk before we go to meet him."

"You're right but I don't know if this is the right time," Ethan said. There was that look on his face that she'd seen before when she'd watched him in court. It was closed off and not showing any emotion. Not at all the man she'd gone to bed with.

"Too bad," she said. She wasn't going to lose Ethan now that she'd found him. She was so close to having the happiness that had always been just out of her reach, and she knew it was centered on him.

She might not understand her feelings for Ethan, but she knew she couldn't just let him walk out the door. She'd waited for years for Mason to come around and he never had. Now it seemed as though he was back from the dead, but that to Crissanne felt like a separate issue. She'd deal with Mason on her own. But first, Ethan.

"I can't do this," Ethan said. "It was one thing to think you'd broken up with him. Then he died, and everything changed. But now he's back…I just feel guilty."

His words cut through her. "Did you never want to be with me for me?"

"What?"

"Is that what you are saying?" she asked. "That it was just sympathy that drove you into my arms? I mean, if that's true then we should have stopped after that day in the conference room."

"That's not what I said," Ethan said, pushing his hands through his hair.

"But is it what you meant? You are way better with words than I am so when you don't say something straight out I have to believe there is a reason for it."

"There is a reason." Ethan turned and almost shouted at her. "I don't want to talk about this. We need to go and see Mason. He's back from the dead. That should be our focus."

"It's not mine," she admitted quietly. "He and I broke up before he died…or was presumed dead. That part of my life was over, and I have to admit being here with you helped me see what was missing between us. I think Mason saw it before I did."

"Great. I'm glad that you are in that place," Ethan said. "I'm not. He knew I always wanted you. He knew that for years I watched you when you were with him."

"That doesn't matter," she said. But she hadn't realized the true extent of how Ethan felt about her while she'd been dating Mason. It changed things in her mind. Had he been with her because she'd been forbidden fruit?

No wonder he didn't want to talk.

But she needed to hear him say that. Ethan had never used her in all the years she'd known him. She didn't want to think that he'd suddenly turned into the kind of man who would now.

"Was I just some tail you'd always wanted?"

"No! You know it's not like that," he said.

But she didn't know anything. The last time she'd made assumptions she lost twelve years of her life to a man who had walked away from her. "What is it like?"

Ethan didn't want to do this. Not now. He was happy Mason wasn't dead, but his timing could have been better. Ethan had finally decided to let his guard down. But now his friend was back and Ethan knew he had to step back and let Mason and Crissanne sort out whatever was between them. No matter what she said.

And she was angling for a fight? What was motivating her here? He tried to see it but with Crissanne his perspective was skewed, as always. He wanted her, he wanted to see what he needed to in her, and that had always made him see her differently.

Now she wanted to know if he thought she was some piece of ass he'd been chasing for twelve years.

"This isn't the time for this kind of discussion," he said. He needed a shower so he could wash the smell of sex and Crissanne off his body, and maybe then he'd be able to think and figure out how to keep her and not betray his friend.

Because every way he sliced this, it looked like a betrayal of Mason.

"This is the only time we have. Mason is on his way to Texas. You want to leave and I don't want you to go without settling this."

"Why?"

She screamed and turned away from him in frustration.

He didn't want to make this night harder on her than it already was. "He's like my brother. He's going to need everyone around him to help him get better. You and I can't go in there all holding hands and whatnot. It's not fair to him."

Crissanne turned back around. She just stared at him for so long that he felt the full weight of her disappointment. "What about what's fair to us?"

"We can talk about that—"

"No. If you can't discuss this with me before... Wait a minute. Do you want to get his approval before you tell him about us?" she asked.

When she put it that way it sounded...well, not like the answer he should be giving her. But the truth was he'd never talked to Mason and gotten his side of the story about the breakup. What if Mason wasn't over Crissanne and would be hurt? They had to figure these things out before they took the next step.

Because what Ethan wanted with Crissanne wasn't just temporary. He had admitted to himself last night that he loved her. But Mason was like a brother, not a man he could just push from his life.

"It's not like that. But it is true he and I never discussed your breakup and he died not knowing you'd come here," Ethan said. "I'm just saying it might be better to ease him into this."

"I agree. I don't want to go in there acting like a couple and make him feel worse than he already does, but I need to know you're by my side," she said. "Are you?"

Was he?

"I am."

"Great," she said, coming to him, putting her arms around him and looking into his eyes.

But he still had that feeling that she was Mason's.

"You can't, can you?" she finally said.

"It's not that I can't be with you, it's that I hate betraying him. Mason saved me when I was heading down a path—"

"You saved yourself, Ethan. You've always been stronger than you gave yourself credit for. Even Mason would say you did it yourself," she said. "You would never have become a drug addict. We both know that."

"I don't know that," Ethan said.

"Why?"

"Because I have an addictive personality."

"Give me an example of this supposed addiction," she said.

"You."

There, he'd said it. "You are the one that I can't forget. That I've watched and wanted for so long. And I think that if I claim you as my own, if I don't give you the space to figure out if Mason's near-death experience has changed him, you might regret it. And then I'd have what I wanted but at a cost I'm not willing to pay."

She put her hands to her hips and took a step back.

"What cost?"

"Your happiness," he said.

He turned away from her and moved a few feet toward the door. He needed to do this not just for Mason but for Crissanne, who very likely might find her feelings for her ex-boyfriend changed now that he was back from the dead.

"I don't think that will happen," she said.

"Neither of us can say for sure what we are going to feel when we see him," Ethan said. His phone pinged and he glanced down at the screen.

"He's at my house. Bart has let him in and set him up in the guest bedroom. Apparently he's in bad shape but is sleeping for now. We need to go," Ethan said.

"Okay then. Let's go. My car was delivered

this week while I was away," she said. "I'll follow you."

He nodded. There was nothing else to say. Not right now. They both needed to go and see Mason. To make sure his friend was okay. And then Ethan could see about this woman who had changed him in a way he hadn't expected to be changed. But he knew if he had to step aside for her to be happy, he would.

That was what love was about, he thought. He remembered his mom reading them a poem when they were young about letting things go and waiting for them to come back. Nate had been sure she meant one of the wild horses that he'd seen on their summer vacation. Ethan hadn't really thought that it made any sense at all. Until this moment, as he followed Crissanne down the stairs out to the parking lot at the end of the block.

It was the wrong time to tell her that he loved her; he knew that. She needed to be able to make her decision unencumbered by that knowledge.

He'd have to let her go and see if she came back.

As Crissanne followed Ethan through town in her new car, she couldn't help thinking that it was all so surreal. She had no idea what had happened, but Mason was back.

She was so happy about the news but didn't

see how it had to change things between her and Ethan. And from how Ethan was acting, she had to wonder if he was more concerned about Mason's happiness than theirs. He'd said he had her feelings front and center at heart, but she wasn't too sure about that.

It felt more like…

She didn't know.

Her radio was playing quietly in the background and when she glanced down to find the volume button, she realized she was crying. What was she going to do?

Mason was alive. Who knew if his crash had changed anything about him? She certainly doubted that after twelve years of her trying to make him into a forever man one crash would be enough to do it. But he'd been through a lot. He may have changed his mind. But so had she. She knew he wasn't the same man who'd left her back in Los Angeles and she had to admit she wasn't the same woman. She'd been afraid to ask him to stay, afraid she wasn't worthy of having a family with him or anyone else. But being with Ethan had given her the strength and the courage to admit that she did want—and deserve—those things.

But she wouldn't know until she saw him. She wiped her nose on the back of her hand as she turned into Ethan's circular drive and parked her car behind his. She took a deep breath, used the hem of her sweatshirt to wipe her entire face dry and then got out of the car, taking the keys with her.

Ethan waited at the top of the stairs on the porch by the front door. Looking at him, she realized she resented him. How he could keep them waiting for a life together even after all they'd built while Mason had supposedly been dead.

She didn't say a word to him when she got to the front door. He looked like he was going to talk, but she just glared him into silence.

The problem with Ethan was that he thought he could explain everything until she just accepted it. And the truth was, that wasn't going to work. Not tonight.

They stepped into the hallway and she had an intense sense of déjà vu from the moment she'd come to Texas after she and Mason had broken up. She'd been looking for a safe place and had found it, not just in this house but in Ethan.

Mason more than likely was thinking the same thing. He was here for Ethan and not for her. She realized that now.

She caught Ethan's arm before he took another step.

"I don't think Mason is here for me," she said at last, her voice sounding thready and raw from the crying she'd done in the car. Mason had already shoved her from his life, and though Ethan thought the three of them would be friends, she just didn't know.

She also didn't know if she could hide the way she felt about him.

She didn't want Ethan to see her the way Mason saw her. As undesirable. Unlovable.

"We won't know until we talk to him," Ethan said.

She nodded. "I just don't want you to see me the way he does. He never wanted me."

Ethan pulled her close and hugged her, and this time she felt a bit of hope that things would sort themselves out. She knew she should step away from him in case Mason got up from the bedroom where Bart had told them he was sleeping. Ethan kissed her temple softly. "I would never see you and not want you."

"How sweet," Mason said from the open doorway of the bedroom downstairs. "I'm left for dead and my girl and my best friend hook up."

Crissanne pulled back and Ethan dropped his arms, turning toward Mason. He had a crutch and one leg in a cast, a sling on his arm, and his nose looked as if it had been broken. His eyes were bloodshot and out of focus.

And she felt her heart take a punch. This man

was broken. She finally understood what Ethan had meant. What Mason needed. She and Ethan went to him at the same time and he just swayed between the two of them.

"I'm so glad you're alive," she said, tears burning her eyes again. God, how had he survived? He looked like he had barely recovered, and this was six weeks after the crash.

"Didn't look like it from where I was," he said.

"Mase, we thought you were dead. Did you really think that the two people who loved you most in this world wouldn't come together to share our grief?" Ethan said, gingerly putting his arm around Mason's middle and leading him back into the bedroom.

"Is that all it was?" Mason asked.

Ethan looked at her and she shrugged. "How did you survive? The production company's people thought you were dead. Everyone assured us that no one survived the crash."

Crissanne rushed ahead to fix the covers. It seemed like Mason had gotten out of the bed in a hurry. Ethan helped him back into it and they got him settled. She took a seat on the end of the bed.

"I was buried under a piece of the wreckage," he said. "I think. I was in and out of consciousness and when I finally woke up I was in a village. They nursed me until I was well enough to be taken down the mountain and transported to a hospital in Lima."

"I'm so glad the villagers found you."

Mason nodded. But his head fell back against the pillows and Crissanne could tell he was far from recovered. This wasn't going to be a quick visit. He'd come to Ethan to recover and she knew that she'd be in the way if she stayed.

"Are they announcing your return in the news?" Ethan asked.

He got the conversation moving on to things they had to discuss.

"Yes. The production company will be sending out the announcement later this morning. They want me to do some press but I wanted to come and find you first... You were like a brother to me," Mason said.

"I still am."

"Doesn't feel like that right now, bro."

"Why did you come here?" Ethan asked. "It's because we are family, right? And you wanted to be with family and not on your own. That hasn't changed."

The two of them were like brothers, and she'd at times realized that her bond with Mason wasn't as strong as the one he shared with Ethan.

Mason seemed to drift to sleep and Ethan looked over at her.

She nodded.

He'd been right. They'd have to wait until Mason was at least more himself before they did anything else.

Crissanne couldn't help feeling that once again the family she'd always craved had been stolen from her.

"I'll take the first watch," he said.

Fourteen

The next two weeks passed slowly for Ethan. October brought with it some fall days, but mostly it stayed warm since it was Texas. The bachelor auction loomed in one week and Mason was starting to recover a bit more. He hadn't said anything to Ethan about Crissanne since that night when he'd first arrived.

Crissanne had been to see Mason several times, and she came over and stayed with him when Ethan had to work long hours. But Ethan and Crissanne had barely had a chance to talk. As glad as he was to have his friend back, he missed

Crissanne. He'd run into her at the coffee shop in town one morning and she'd looked tired and so pretty he hadn't been able to think of anything but kissing her and holding her in his arms.

Mason had gone to Houston for a day to do a satellite uplink and interviews with all of the morning news shows. Otherwise he was lying low in Cole's Hill until he finished healing and figured out his next move.

Ethan didn't know where that left Mason and Crissanne so he had been giving her space. But he wanted her back in his life. And he had no idea how to ask if she and Mason were back together.

So he'd stared at her awkwardly before turning and leaving the shop without his coffee. At work his assistant said he'd turned into a tyrant and had assured him that unless he changed his attitude he wasn't going to get any bids at the bachelor auction.

Carlene had a point. Ethan knew that he had to figure out how to go back to the old way he'd always been around Mason and Crissanne. But he couldn't. Back then, he'd never held her in his arms, let alone kissed her or made love to her.

"Dude, did you hear a thing I said?" Mason asked, interrupting his thoughts. They were sitting at the table near Ethan's pool playing twenty-one. They were supposed to be figuring out how to legally bring Mason back from the dead. It wasn't easy. There was a lot of paperwork. Ethan was still working to get everything filed and then expedited.

"Sorry. My mind was elsewhere," he replied. "What'd you say?"

"What's up with you and Crissanne?"

"Nothing," Ethan said.

"Did Derek tell you that lying to me would speed up my recovery?" Mason asked as he put his cards on the table and leaned forward, putting his arms on the table.

"Derek is a cardiologist. Even if he had I wouldn't believe him," Ethan said.

"Well, I'm not blind," Mason said. "You two are damned awkward around each other, and that's telling."

Ethan shrugged. "I don't want to talk about her."

"You never have," Mason agreed. "Even when I asked her out to make you jealous."

"Is that why you asked her out?" Ethan asked. He'd never thought much about it. Why wouldn't Mason want Crissanne? From the moment he'd seen her with her blond hair and her stormy gray eyes, Ethan had wanted her.

"Maybe. I mean, that's not why I stayed with her for twelve years," Mason said.

"But you broke up, right? That's what she said."

Mason rubbed his hand over his chest and shifted back in his chair. "We did. I...I wasn't ready to commit the way she wanted. She wants kids and a family."

Ethan felt the sharp sting of jealousy at the thought of Crissanne and Mason having kids together. He wasn't going to be able to save his friendship with Mason. He just wasn't. And as much as he loved the other man like a brother, if he and Crissanne got back together it would be torture for Ethan. He had thought he could be noble and put her happiness first, but that would be the end of this.

"She deserves it," Ethan said. "She'd never even had her own place until she leased the studio and apartment in Cole's Hill."

"I know. I thought...we're so similar, Cris and I. But she grew up holding on to dreams of what might be and I grew up secure in the knowledge that family was the kind of messed-up tie I never wanted."

For the first time since he'd come back to Cole's Hill, Mason sounded like his old self.

"I thought my mom had changed your mind."

He shook his head. "Nah, your family is the exception that proves the rule. But Cris never saw that."

"Do you want her back?" he asked.

"She's not yours to give," Mason said. "Or mine to take. I think we both know she'd light into us but good if she heard us discussing her like this."

"I know," Ethan said. "But you changed after almost dying…in a lot of ways. I've never seen you this mellow before."

Mason took off his sunglasses and Ethan searched his green gaze for an answer to the question he didn't want to ask. Had Mason decided that he wanted a family now that he'd almost died? But there was no answer in his eyes.

"That might be the drugs I'm using to manage my pain," Mason said.

But Ethan knew his friend better than that. He had changed in a fundamental way. He'd been very clear about wanting to live here in Cole's Hill instead of going back to Los Angeles. That was a huge change, and Ethan suspected it had a lot to do with him wanting to be closer to family. His family, and of course, Crissanne.

If Mason tried to get her back, hell, he would win. Ethan couldn't take a chance at happiness from him or Crissanne after they'd waited twelve years for it.

"I hurt her, Eth. I said things that I knew would hurt her and I don't think she could ever forgive that."

"Why did you do it?"

"Because she deserved more than me. You asked if I'd changed and the truth is sort of a vague maybe. I don't know yet. When I see you and Crissanne together I want her, but that's because I'm selfish and don't want you to have everything. I've always been jealous of you because of your brothers and your family, even this town you live in. If you had the woman you always wanted…well, I won't say any more and show you just how much of a bastard I can be."

Mason's honesty humbled him and he got up and went around the table to hug his friend. "You have all of this. My family is yours. My town is yours."

"And Crissanne?"

"Is her own woman," Crissanne said, startling the both of them as she walked out onto the patio.

Crissanne had been in town buying some clothes and shaving items for Mason that he'd asked her to get for him. It had become clear over the last two weeks that she and Mason had fallen into a new pattern. The spark that had once flared between them was gone. It had been gone for a while; that's why they'd broken up. But in its place there was something new.

More of a friendship, and she liked it. She was

getting closer to thinking that she might be able to find her way back to Ethan with each day that Mason spent in recovery. She knew she'd fallen fast for Ethan, given that she'd been with Mason for a dog's age and hadn't ever felt like this.

"Mason, you and I were over as a couple long before I forced the confrontation and we broke up. Thinking you were dead made me realize how much I care for you but I have to be honest, those feelings aren't the same as what I feel for Ethan."

"Fair enough," Mason said. "But I know that neither of you has mentioned the thing that I said that first night. That you two are clearly more than friends now."

Ethan stood up. "The time hasn't been right to discuss anything. Your recovery is the top priority."

"That's very nice of you," he said, sounding slightly sarcastic.

"It's the truth," Crissanne insisted.

Mason looked at her and his expression softened. "I know. I was jealous and also a little sad because we never had what I saw between you two," he said to her. "I know that I've thrown everything up in the air between you and that's the last thing I'd want for the two people who matter the most to me in this world."

Mason stood up and walked to Ethan, using

his crutch. "I know that neither of you is mine to give away to the other but I'm taking myself out of this equation. Just know we're always going to be friends no matter what happens."

He walked by them and into the house. Ethan turned toward Crissanne, who just watched him go. Ethan had no idea what to say. And when he looked at Crissanne he realized that she didn't know, either. She stood there with one arm around her waist, her sunglasses pushed up on the top of her head.

"I love you," he said. "Before we say anything else I need you to know that. I thought I could step aside and do whatever I need to in order to make sure you were happy, but I realized that I can't. I want you in my life. I want to start a family with you."

"Ethan—"

"Let me finish," he said. "I know that I was pushing to give us time to figure this out but if I'm being honest, being apart from you has just made me realize how clear my feelings are. All the doubts I had are gone. I know it's not fair to throw this at you right now. That Mason is still recovering and no matter what he said, you have a right to your feelings. I'll wait but you should know that I'm not going to be standing on the sidelines while you figure out what you want. I'm going to do everything I can to show you how much I love you and how perfect our life together can be."

She walked toward him. "Perfect is an illusion. In real life, there aren't filters to blur away the rough edges, and you know what, Ethan? I'm so glad. Because I love you, too. I mean, I never in my entire life felt anything for a person close to what I feel for you. I've been trying to give you the space you needed to work things out with Mason, but I miss you.

"Every night I hug that pillow you slept on at my loft close to my chest and pretend it's you. Every morning I'm at the coffee shop in town hoping you'll stop in for a cup before work just to see you, because even if we don't talk it makes my day a little better to simply see you."

"Really?" he asked.

"Truly," she said.

He pulled her into his arms and kissed her because the only other words he had to say were jumbled in his head. He didn't want to start babbling like an idiot and was very much afraid he would.

"I want to marry you," he said.

"Yes. I want that, too."

"Good. We can start with you moving back in with me," he said.

"Okay," she said. Her heart was so full of love

and happiness that she was almost afraid to trust it, but then Ethan lifted her in his arms and carried her toward the house, and she knew that she'd found safety with him. He was the one person she could trust to always be there for her.

Epilogue

With the bachelor auction in full swing, Crissanne left her position backstage to make her way to the front of the ballroom. Mason was saving her a seat at the Caruthers family table; it was funny how the two of them had realized that they had the family they both had always been seeking. She sat between Kinley's nanny and Mason, ready to bid on her man.

Crissanne was wearing a simple engagement ring that Ethan had given her the night before at a family dinner at his parents' house. She glanced at it as she sat down and Mason winked at her. "You two are perfect together. Almost makes me think about finding someone of my own."

She doubted that would ever happen. "What woman could compete with the wildness of a mountain path you have yet to climb?"

"Touché."

Pa Caruthers said something to Mason and he turned away. Pippa flipped through the catalog as if she were looking for someone.

"Are you bidding tonight?" Crissanne asked her.

"I am. I've had my eye on this Texan for a while," she said, pointing to Diego Velasquez. "And since it's my birthday I've decided to treat myself."

Crissanne laughed at the way the other woman said it. "He's certainly a treat. And flirty as all get out. I think you'll have fun with him."

"Good," Pippa said. "I need some fun in my life."

Before she could respond, Nate, who was emceeing the event, announced Ethan's name. Crissanne turned toward the front of the room as her fiancé walked out toward the center of the stage. The emcee was reading a bio about Ethan, and Crissanne noticed it wasn't the one that had been in the brochure.

"Ethan Caruthers was the last of the wild Caruthers boys to remain single, and some say it was because he was waiting for the right woman to come along. Of course, the bidding is open to anyone, but Ethan has warned us that his heart and soul belong to only one woman and his wild days are behind him. So he's made a large contribution to make up for the bids and has asked that we offer him up only to the one who truly loves him and wants to spend the rest of her life with him."

"I do!" Crissanne said, jumping up and raising her hand.

"Come and claim your bachelor," Nate said.

Ethan met her halfway to the stage, pulling her into his arms and kissing her. There was applause and whoops of joy. She put her hand on his face as he lifted his head. "You're mine."

"Always," he said.

"And now for our next bachelor," the emcee persisted from the stage. "Ladies, prepare to be tempted by the untamable Diego Velasquez."

* * * * *

As the bachelor auction heats up,
who will be the highest bidder
for Diego Velasquez?

Find out in

Rancher Untamed

by USA TODAY *bestselling author*
Katherine Garbera

Available October 2018
from Harlequin Desire.

***

If you're on Twitter, tell us what you think of
Harlequin Desire! #harlequindesire

COMING NEXT MONTH FROM

HARLEQUIN *Desire*

Available September 4, 2018

#2611 KEEPING SECRETS
Billionaires and Babies • by Fiona Brand
Billionaire Damon Smith's sexy assistant shared his bed and then vanished for a year. Now she's returned—with his infant daughter! Can he work through the dark secrets Zara's still hiding and claim the family he never knew he wanted?

#2612 RUNAWAY TEMPTATION
Texas Cattleman's Club: Bachelor Auction
by Maureen Child
When Caleb attends a colleague's wedding, the last person he expects to leave with is the runaway bride! He offers Shelby a temporary hideout on his ranch. But soon the sizzle between them has this wealthy cowboy wondering if seduction will convince her to stay...

#2613 STRANGER IN HIS BED
The Masters of Texas • by Lauren Canan
Brooding Texan Wade Masters brings his estranged wife home from the hospital with amnesia. This new, sensual, *kind* Victoria makes him feel things he never has before. But when he discovers the explosive truth, will their second chance at love be as doomed as their first?

#2614 ONE NIGHT SCANDAL
The McNeill Magnates • by Joanne Rock
Actress Hannah must expose the man who hurt her sister. Sexy rancher Brock has clues, but amnesia means he can't remember them—or his one night with her! Still, he pursues her with a focus she can't resist. What happens when he finds out everything?

#2615 THE RELUCTANT HEIR
The Jameson Heirs • by HelenKay Dimon
Old-money heir Carter Jameson has a family who thrives on deceit. He's changing that by finding the woman who knows devastating secrets about his father. The problem? He wants her, maybe more than he wants redemption. And what he thinks she knows is nothing compared to the truth...

#2616 PLAYING MR. RIGHT
Switching Places • by Kat Cantrell
CEO Xavier LeBlanc must resist his new employee—his inheritance is on the line! But there's more to her than meets the eye...because she's working undercover to expose fraud at his charity. Too bad Xavier is falling faster than her secrets are coming to light...

HDCNM0818

Get 4 FREE REWARDS!

We'll send you 2 FREE Books plus 2 FREE Mystery Gifts.

Harlequin® Desire books feature heroes who have it all: wealth, status, incredible good looks... everything but the right woman.

FREE Value Over **$20**

YES! Please send me 2 FREE Harlequin® Desire novels and my 2 FREE gifts (gifts are worth about $10 retail). After receiving them, if I don't wish to receive any more books, I can return the shipping statement marked "cancel." If I don't cancel, I will receive 6 brand-new novels every month and be billed just $4.55 per book in the U.S. or $5.24 per book in Canada. That's a savings of at least 13% off the cover price! It's quite a bargain! Shipping and handling is just 50¢ per book in the U.S. and 75¢ per book in Canada*. I understand that accepting the 2 free books and gifts places me under no obligation to buy anything. I can always return a shipment and cancel at any time. The free books and gifts are mine to keep no matter what I decide.

225/326 HDN GMYU

Name (please print)

Address   Apt. #

City   State/Province   Zip/Postal Code

Mail to the **Reader Service:**
IN U.S.A.: P.O. Box 1341, Buffalo, NY 14240-8531
IN CANADA: P.O. Box 603, Fort Erie, Ontario L2A 5X3

Want to try two free books from another series? Call 1-800-873-8635 or visit www.ReaderService.com.

*Terms and prices subject to change without notice. Prices do not include applicable taxes. Sales tax applicable in N.Y. Canadian residents will be charged applicable taxes. Offer not valid in Quebec. This offer is limited to one order per household. Books received may not be as shown. Not valid for current subscribers to Harlequin Desire books. All orders subject to approval. Credit or debit balances in a customer's account(s) may be offset by any other outstanding balance owed by or to the customer. Please allow 4 to 6 weeks for delivery. Offer available while quantities last.

Your Privacy—The Reader Service is committed to protecting your privacy. Our Privacy Policy is available online at www.ReaderService.com or upon request from the Reader Service. We make a portion of our mailing list available to reputable third parties that offer products we believe may interest you. If you prefer that we not exchange your name with third parties, or if you wish to clarify or modify your communication preferences, please visit us at www.ReaderService.com/consumerchoice or write to us at Reader Service Preference Service, P.O. Box 9062, Buffalo, NY 14240-9062. Include your complete name and address.

HD18

Shelby Arthur stared at her own reflection and hardly
recognized herself. She supposed all brides felt like
that on their wedding day, but for her, the effect was
terrifying.

She was looking at a stranger wearing an old-fashioned
gown with long, lacy sleeves, a cinched waist and full
skirt, and a neckline that was so high she felt as if she
were choking. Shelby was about to get married in a dress
she hated, a veil she didn't want, to a man she wasn't sure
she liked, much less loved. How did she get to this point?

"Oh, God. What am I doing?"

She'd left her home in Chicago to marry Jared
Goodman. But now that he was home in Texas, under
his awful father's thumb, Jared was someone she didn't

even know. Her whirlwind romance had morphed into a nightmare and now she was trapped.

Shelby met her own eyes in the mirror and read the desperation there. In a burst of fury, she ripped her veil off her face. Then, blowing a stray auburn lock from her forehead, she gathered up the skirt of the voluminous gown in both arms and hurried down the hall and toward the nearest exit.

And ran smack into a brick wall.

Well, that was what it felt like.

A tall, gorgeous brick wall who grabbed her upper arms to steady her, then smiled down at her with humor in his eyes. He had enough sex appeal to light up the city of Houston, and the heat from his hands, sliding down her body, made everything inside her jolt into life.

"Aren't you headed the wrong way?" he asked, and the soft drawl in his deep voice awakened a single thought in her mind.

Oh, boy.

Don't miss
Runaway Temptation
by USA TODAY *bestselling author Maureen Child,*
the first in the Texas Cattleman's Club:
Bachelor Auction series.

Available September 2018 wherever
Harlequin® Desire books and ebooks are sold.

www.Harlequin.com

Want to give in to temptation with
steamy tales of irresistible desire?

Check out **Harlequin® Presents®,
Harlequin® Desire** and
Harlequin® Kimani™ Romance books!

New books available every month!